To Mom, Dad, MTTJJ

To my Twitch community and friends

*To Toria,
for keeping my creative spirit alive*

Copyright © 2021 Luella White

All rights reserved.

Paperback ISBN: 9798707822056

Edited by Robin Rose Graves
Cover art by Victoria May

Printed by Amazon.com in the USA

Chapter 1

Now, I'll remind you, my friend, that the street was silent as the dead. A sound in the dark would have been an assault to anyone's calm mind. The girl in the heavy coat was no exception to this.

"Who's there?" she whispered, her words dissolving in the cold air. Other words escaped her mind as two beings appeared in the dim light of the lamp above them. One figure growled viciously-a canine-while the other simply smiled until his entire face looked to be split in half, only a few manually sharpened teeth visible in his mouth. His stance resembled that of a hunch-backed ape's, walking on both his hands and his feet.

Pop-pop. Snap.

Romilla realized that the disturbing sound came from the joints of the smiling creature as it walked. Paralyzed with horror, she gripped the iron rail next to her. The plastered smile on the corpse spilled forth a clumsy greeting.

"Come now, Verdorben here doesn't bite."

Her insides shook with the cold and the fear. Romilla watched as the drooling dog stepped next to the smiling thing. She cleared her already dry throat. Every instinct she had told her to run, run far away. But instead, she used this pause to speak.

"Who are you?" she asked, an accent dotting her words. The smiling thing and the wolf both tilted their heads.

"No one of any importance," the creature hissed, a long, thin tongue protruding from between the gaps of its teeth as it spoke. "Until the world is in dire need of us, then we'll arrive."

Romilla pursed her lips. She scrutinized the hunched backs, the grotesquely bony flesh, the patches of rotted fur, and the long strings of hair that fell to the smiling creature's elbows. Disgusted, she forced herself to look away. As soon as she looked up again, the two creatures were gone.

Romilla's heart started to race, the adrenaline immediately starting to warm her nearly frozen body. She shook her head.

"I've gone mad," she mumbled to herself, in a vain attempt to come up with an excuse for the gruesome sight. She released her grip from the iron rail, not realizing that, rather than melting away the cold layer around it, she'd formed a layer of ice where her hand was. Before she could relax, each of the lamps went out, one by one.

"No-!" she cried.

Cruelly, the snow fell heavier after the street's lights went out. Romilla's breath caught in her throat. Perhaps this was all just a dream. A wild, horrific dream. Dream or not, the girl ran. Whatever direction she moved in didn't matter; as long as she could find the secure sanctuary of light. Perched atop a building, the two creatures watched as the girl pushed herself through the heavy snow. The human corpse clicked his tongue as Romilla trudged past where they sat. The wolf appeared suddenly in front of the girl, causing her to stumble backwards. Thick slobber dribbled from between the carnivorous teeth.

"P-please," Romilla whispered, her voice barely a crack. "Please, let me pass."

Verdorben replied by taking a few steps closer. The girl retreated as carefully as she could, not taking her eyes away from the black and bony wolf. Two snaky eyes appeared behind it, through the heavy snowflakes.

"I-I mean no harm," Romilla stammered, unsure of what else to say. "I'll leave. Please, I'll leave."

Verdorben growled, his thin muscles twitching. The smiling corpse faced his companion, pulled back his bone of an arm, and slashed the wolf's side with his claws.

Having been provoked, the wolf lunged for Romilla. Before the girl had a chance to react, the wolf had forced itself on her, using its claws and teeth to attempt to rip away at her arms and chest and stomach. With one free arm, the girl threw a fresh icicle at the hound's forehead, causing him to topple off of her. She scrambled to her feet, blindly running away.

"Not sssso fast," the humanoid whispered, sinking into the ground as a shadow and appearing in front of Romilla, who fell back into the hard cobble road. The thing swung his hands back and forth, making her face and neck a painted array of red stripes. She buried her face into the snow with a cry of pain. Before anything else could happen, she lifted a round barrier of ice out of the ground around her. The corpse pounded on it, screeching and cursing.

"Break it!" he shouted at his pet. Verdorben charged headfirst through the dome of ice, shattering it and landing hard on Romilla. She let out another strained scream as the wolf pinned her down on both arms, black drool dripping on her face. The smiling creature stood on her legs, licking his non-existent lips. Romilla opened her mouth, releasing a thick cloud of icy fog. With this distraction, the girl shoved the two creatures off of her and stumbled back on to her feet.

As she stood up, the corpse seized her arm. He pulled her horribly close to his face and punctured her arm with his claws. She tugged and pulled to break free, but somehow the clammy corpse, despite a distinct lack of muscle, yanked her back with brute force.

"No, please!!"

The pain shot up the girl's arm and throughout the body as the thing's claws dug deeper into her skin. She grimaced and sank to the ground, her voice nothing more than a high-pitched sobbing.

"Cold-blooded," the thing hissed. "Soon to change."

Romilla could feel the blood oozing through the gashes in her arms, dripping around the corpse's claws. Something burst underneath her skin and into her veins. The girl only yelped, yanking her arm free and watching in the dim light as her skin started to blacken.

"No-!" she choked.

The humanoid cackled, stepping back to watch as the girl descended into despair. Verdorben licked his chops, panting heavily with primal hunger.

Pain seeped into the girl's head like an intrusive smoky haze. Everything blurred around her.

"Please, please, don't . . ." she whispered. The smiling thing took her neck in his cold hands.

"Too late, we've killed you, my dear."

One final pulse of pain erupted within the girl's chest. She cried out and threw herself into the snow, face-down, as everything she knew came to a complete halt.

Verdorben loomed over at the collapsed girl, his hot breath enough to melt her dry skin. The corpse licked his teeth with a snaky tongue. With limited strength, he turned the girl onto her back. An extremely dim blue light appeared from behind her eyes through her ragged coat, only to slowly start fading away. He grinned with satisfaction as the light simmed, into oblivion. To its death.

"Now, Verdorben," he whispered, running a claw down the body's thin, pale arm, "we feast."

Just as both creatures had opened their mouths to sink their teeth into their freshest kill, the sound of approaching carriage wheels and hoof beats met their ears (or, what was left of them). The corpse let out an irritated hissing sound, and the two beasts slithered into the ground as shadows, leaving the body of Romilla behind.

And yet, they hadn't noticed the little blue light making a slight appearance once again as shuddering breaths slowly left her mouth.

It would seem that they hadn't killed her after all, my friend.

Chapter 2

Only I could hold down that many drinks without turning into a complete fool. My darling nephew, however, shone in ways I'd never seen after drinking so much. His tie and brooch fell victim to the young ladies that admired him as much as some of the others admired me. Ah, I'd taught him well. I soon lost track of my nephew once a striking blonde perched herself in my lap and crooned sweet nothings to me.

Yes, me-Shandar Vrana. The eldest of the two Vrana brothers, though regrettably not as rich as my brother. That's why I live with him. Many women describe me as adventurous and alluring as the mythical Odysseus, though much thinner in build and likely far better dressed. With snowy pale skin, long and rich dark hair reaching my back, thick arched eyebrows, and slightly drooping eyes that can gaze seductively into your soul - that would be me. Shandar Vrana.

"Your clothing is plenty fascinating to me," she said. I put a hand on her neck, stroking the thin chain around it. "Your lacy cravat, your pearly cuff links, your luxurious hair...are you royalty?"

"Darling, with you at my side, I could be king," I said. Such sweet words could bring a woman to her knees with anticipation, as I'd learned. That said, I continued. "Or, if you'd like, I could be yours."

I carefully wove my hand around her skirt and found her leg.

"You've already conquered my attention, sir. What's your name?"

"I should like to hear it on your lips," I said. "My name-"

No sooner had I spoken when I heard shouting coming from the other end of the pub. A casual glance revealed my nephew in the midst of an argument with the pub's owner. Realizing that I was responsible for the boy, I cursed and called his name.

"Sullivan!"

"Oh, never mind that little scuffle," the blonde insisted. She turned my head back to face hers. "What did you say your name was?"

I opened my mouth to reply, only to look again as I heard something shatter. The owner held a broken bottle, and my nephew collapsed from the impact.

"Damn it, you little-"

I shoved the blonde off of my lap and rushed to my nephew's side.

"This filthy rat is yours?" the large man asked, pointing the remains of his bottle at Sullivan. My eyes darted around as we caught the attention of everyone in the pub.

"He's a...ah, a close friend's son," I lied.

"Oh, 'e is?"

"Yes, yes." Sullivan began to stir. "Do not speak, you've caused a scene," I hissed into the boy's ear.

"'Well, tell your friend that 'is son is a lying, thieving little bastard!" the man spat. "Not a penny shown for the drinks he's had!"

"Ah, my apologies, sir; he's still young," I stammered. My nephew was no longer unconscious, but his weight felt dead nonetheless. I attempted to lift him up, back to his feet. Why couldn't he be thin and spindly like me?

"Show me the money; no excuses or you'll be next!"

It wasn't the first time I'd been threatened, but the man was rather formidable - large, muscly, bushy mustache. A force that wasn't to be reckoned with. I fished a fair sum from my pockets and set it on the table.

"Now, you get that boy out of me pub-and don't let me see 'im here again!"

I nodded, eyeing the rest of the patrons as they held back chuckles. My nephew let out a groan before letting out a foolish battle cry.

"Fight me like a man, you old buffoon!" he slurred.

"Enough, boy!" I hissed as the rest of the pub shot

angry or amused stares at us. I continued to drag the young man out of the door. "We're going home."

I dragged him through the pub and noticed the blonde smirking at me as she seduced a different, much less attractive patron than myself.

"What a cowardly old bastard with bastard children and bastard women!" Sullivan yelled, presumably directed towards the barkeep. I slammed the door shut behind me and took a sharp breath of the cold Asterbury air. Thankfully, the rest of the city seemed quiet.

"Why so soon, Uncle Shandar?" the boy whined, stumbling back towards the doors. I used a single arm to pull him back.

"All good things must come to an end, my dear nephew," I said bitterly. "Even through an interference beyond your control." I suddenly realized the boy was shivering. "Where's your coat?"

The guilty look on his face indicated that his coat was still inside.

"Never mind, wear this," I huffed as I took my own furs off and wrapped them around the boy. "Get into the coach, Sullivan."

"Charles, Charles!" the boy shouted to our coachman and butler. "Charles, bring me to the nearest harlot, if you would!"

Charles looked at me disapprovingly. I shook my head.

"You know where to bring us, my good man," I said, dropping a few coins into his hand. I leaned in as I did. "And here's a little extra to keep quiet when we arrive."

Charles nodded, ignoring my nephew's drunken fit. How strange that I recalled being his age, not having a care in the world, hardly being responsible for my own actions. I also recalled that blonde, whom I would have been pleasuring now had it not been for my nephew. That'd teach me for bringing him along with me. Eventually, the boy collapsed in an exhausted, drunken heap as we rattled along the roads of the city.

I myself began to doze off, when Charles abruptly brought the coach to a halt. Both Sullivan and I lurched forward, waking us both up.

"Uncle..?"

He sounded more sober now, at least.

"Charles, what's happened?" I shouted. When he didn't answer, I looked out of the window to see ahead. A few constables stood around something under a single lamp. "Wait here, Sullivan."

As I stepped out and moved closer, I realized that they weren't standing around some*thing*, but some*one*. A hand stopped me from moving any further, grabbing my shoulder.

"Apologies, sir, but no civilians are to step any closer. This girl has been horribly wounded."

I took another look at the poor creature, to catch a glimpse of how injured she was. In the dim light, it was difficult, though not impossible, to see the gruesomely dark patches of snow around her.

"How awful," I mumbled. There wasn't much else for me to say with a churning stomach.

"Indeed. We're taking her to the doctor, in the hopes she can be saved. Lord only knows what kind of creature attempted to rip her to shreds."

My insides turned violently as I heard a faint gurgling coming from the girl's mouth. I shuddered, pulling my vest tighter around my body.

"Uncle Shandar?"

Sullivan appeared behind me.

"Damn it, Sullivan, I thought I told you to wait in the coach!"

The boy's wide eyes didn't focus on me, however. The sight of a ghostly girl covered in blood would draw anyone's eyes, I supposed. I decided not to press the matter, it served him right.

"What's happened?" he asked, his speech still a slur.

"Something attacked her, though it's not certain what."

My nephew stared as the group of men lifted the delicate girl.

"And...and she's still alive?"

"To my knowledge, although perhaps not for much longer."

A biting gust of wind blew powdery snow from the fences and the lamps and into our faces. When the wind subsided, I noticed where she had placed her own gaze-on my nephew and I. It shocked me to see her mouth moving the instant she noticed us, though no one could hear what she was saying. If she hadn't vanished out of the light in the arms of the policemen, I'd have thought she was silently calling to us for help. The eerie idea hung in the air, filling me with a dread I'd never thought to feel before.

"Come along, lad," I said, rushing the boy back to the carriage through my discomfort. "'Tis nothing to be afraid of."

At the time, I refused to accept that what I'd said was for my own reassurance.

My brother's home, a previously abandoned and dismal war fortress that he and his wife had taken the liberty of fixing up, sat on the outskirts of the city, close to the thick and daunting Reditum forest. It held the same charm as a graveyard in the middle of the night. As we approached, I executed my plan of bringing the boy into the house without his parents becoming an obstacle. I'd imagine they were worried sick about their son. I had to play the fool and act like I hadn't seen him all night.

"Don't let his father or mother see him," I said to Charles, slipping him a few more coins. "Perhaps 'round the back, through the kitchen. I'll go through the front, to avoid suspicion."

"I'm afraid that the suspicions of Master Halvard and Miss Violet Ann are the last of your worries," Charles mumbled. "Considering they don't suspect, they *know*."

"Remember your place, Charles, or your little bonus must be returned. I'm aware of what I'm doing."

"Begging your pardon, sir," the butler growled. "Come this way, Sullivan. Let's get you to bed."

As they disappeared into the darkness around the corner of the building, I decided to let myself in through the front. A young maid, Lizabet, answered the door as I knocked.

"You're dreadfully late, Master Shandar," she murmured as she took my gloves and heavy vest. "It's a quarter past two."

"If I wanted the time, I would consult a clock, Lizabet," I snapped as I dug the remaining coins out of my pocket and dropped them into her palm. "Keep it between us, my dear."

The girl pursed her lips, knowing full well the consequences of her actions.

"Will that be all, Master Shandar?" she asked reluctantly as the coins trickled into her apron pocket.

"A cup of tea to my room will be my last request tonight," I said, starting my ascent up the stairs. "Cream and sugar, if you will, please."

I felt the insides of my now-empty pockets and my thoughts returned to the blonde in the pub. What a lovely sight she was. Oh, but what a young and naive fool my nephew was, making my carefree life nothing but a chore. That woman's face - so perfectly painted. And her hair so perfectly curled and played up. I felt myself smiling at the memory of just touching her.

Two legs dressed in black interrupted my daydream. My little brother, Sullivan's father, the esteemed and more-than-comfortably retired merchant, Master Halvard Vrana, stared down at me from the top stair with folded arms and a lightly creased face. His dark hair, lit up with the streaks of grey, ended just above his shoulders. I much preferred my own dark, wavy locks that fell to my upper back. I frequently made our hair length into a competition, though he never played along with me.

"Home late again, Shandar."

I chuckled and went up to match his eye level, putting a hand on his shoulder.

"For you, Halvard," I said. "Though I personally prefer 'fashionably late'."

"Nonetheless," Halvard snapped at me. "Where is Sullivan? I've not seen him all night, and his mother is worried." Even I wasn't sure at that point. Perhaps the boy laid in the middle of a corridor, ill.

"In bed, I'd imagine," I lied, despite the thought. "Soundly sleeping, happy as a lark."

"Violet and I haven't seen him since earlier this evening."

At dinner, I'd assume. That was the last I'd seen of him, as well. Sober, at least.

"Nor I, and yet you ask me," I answered.

"You were with him."

I couldn't help it if the boy enjoyed long talks in the snowy garden with his dear old uncle.

"This afternoon, yes."

"Did he say he was going anywhere?"

"He said nothing of the kind."

I'm the one who offered.

"You invited him along, then?"

Spot-on, unfortunately. I had to work my way around this.

"And if I did? Is he not old enough to make his own decisions, Halvard?"

"I'd rather him be making intelligent decisions than stooping to your level, Shandar."

"Well, fortunately for you, he's likely made the decision to go to bed," I said. "A rather smart choice, if I do say so myself."

I brushed past my little brother as I watched Lizabet turn the corner of the hallway with my tray of tea.

"I've made the same decision," I announced with a false yawn. "You'd best follow my example, Halvard. Tell your bonny wife not to worry. Good night!"

I walked into my room and Lizabet followed behind me, looking warily at the master of the household before she did. Halvard went off, seething; I knew this too well, his temper flared but his composure remained quiet. Lucky for me, he didn't follow me and stormed his way down the stairs.

"Close the door behind you, Lizabet," I said. "And thank you for the tea."

"My pleasure," she replied before shutting the door. I laid back in my bed and dropped to sleep before I could sip at my hot drink.

Chapter 3

Nighttime surrounded the grand city of Asterbury, and the two creatures swimming through the shadows cautiously checked the streets for a meal.

"Tired of birds and skinny fawns and rats," Petimus mumbled to his pet. Verdorben let out a snort. "I crave more, like in the times of old. We feasted like kings in those days, did we not?"

Verdorben replied with a hollow sneeze. The creatures both emerged from the ground of the empty alley they stood in. For you see, Petimus thought he smelt something delectable there. Lo and behold, before them laid a child, shivering and covered with a torn coat, in a bed of rubbish. Petimus chuckled to himself and assumed the position – a cripple in the dark, cloaked with a blanket of shadow to appear like a clothed human. Verdorben let out a routine growl as Petimus leaned against the wall.

"Now, now," the corpse creature recited. "No need for you to get defensive, my sweet pup." The child stood up in alarm. He could only see two faint outlines across from him in the dirty alley.

"I'm...please forgive me, sir," he said sheepishly, backing away from the creatures. "Please don't take me to the workhouse, please." Petimus chuckled and pulled Verdorben closer to him. The wolf sat down next to him.

"Don't suppose you'd have a penny for a poor beggar, or a bone for me cur?" The boy shook his head.

"'Fraid not, sir," he answered. Petimus took a better look at the boy. Skinny, but old enough to be able-bodied. Perhaps twelve or thirteen.

"Come now, no need to be frightened," the beggar said. "Come closer. Though I may not have much, there is a life I can offer. A job, if you will." The poor child stepped up to the end of the alley, where he saw what seemed to be a poor man with a blanket draped over him and a dog, lying down at the man's feet.

"A better life than this?" the child asked naively.

"Oh, far better, lad," Petimus said with a hidden sly grin. "I don't suppose you're a strong lad?"

"S-Strong as my bones allow, sir."

"And you're not crippled, like the poor wretch here before you?"

"N-no sir."

Petimus nodded. "Well, you've already passed my test, then, my child," he said. "Let me touch those arms, how strong they are." The boy held out his hand cautiously. Upon feeling the rotting skin touch his own rosy flesh, he let out a cry. Verdorben jumped up and snarled at him while Petimus' strong grip remained a challenge to break free from. "Then let us proceed to my home," Petimus said among the sniffling and sputtering of the scared child. "Nalia will love a hearty young man like yourself to be added to her collection." Before the poor boy could scream for help, Petimus placed a hand over his mouth and pierced his skin with sharp claw-like nails. Black flowed down into the boy's chest until the life from his eyes drained and his heart stopped its beating. "Will be a soft and delicious meal, Verdorben," Petimus said. "A meal well deserved, I think. Come, Verdorben, let us go home."

As they trekked through the woods, blood fresh in their teeth, Petimus recited his favorite poem.

"Beware the beggar, little one, beware his sharpened gaze..."

The rhythm of the poem almost matched the sound of bones struggling to be mobile.

Pop-pop. Snap. Pop-pop. Snap.

"Beware his eyes, like a hungry sssnake..."

Pop-pop. Snap.

*"And his touch, like torn lace...*Oh, Verdorben, my touch is not anything like lace," Petimus mumbled to his pup

as they both sauntered through the coniferous forest on four legs. "More of a...a dead and drying decaying fish."

The thing cackled as they approached the center of the Reditum forest, trudging through the snow. No path showed them where they walked to, and nothing lit the way. Petimus and Verdorben, you see, lived in this forest. They could tell every conifer tree apart from each other, as well as every large rock, rabbit hole, and little frozen brooks and streams. After taking a turn at the thick dead tree trunk, Petimus and Verdorben approached the campfire pit next to a crudely made yet sturdy little hut.

"Wonder if she's anything else for us to eat," Petimus said, examining the cooking spit and pot above the campfire. "Perhaps inside."

Just as he touched the door, a crow let out a raspy and loud squawk. It flew overhead, startling the two creatures that stood there.

"Ah, and here she is," Petimus crooned as the crow turned and started to swoop past them again. With unmatched precision, Verdorben jumped and caught the bird in its mandibles, shaking it to death once he landed.

"You'll make a lovely dinner," the corpse said to the mangled crow, licking what should have been his lips.

"Little wretch!"

Both of the creatures looked up to see an old, gray-haired woman in the doorway of the hut. She stared them down with harsh, wild eyes. One might only see these types of eyes in the cell of an asylum. The only thing different about these brown eyes with drooping eyelids was that, every once in a while, an observer could see hints of black crawling through the irises like tiny worms.

"Nalia," Petimus greeted, "my sister of the shadow."

"Still your tongue," the woman snapped, reaching for the dead and bloody bird. "This is mine."

Petimus and Verdorben both whined as the woman picked up the creature and cradled it in her arms, cooing to it like it were a baby. A dead, bleeding baby.

"Poor dear, have you been mauled? Mangled? The abyss is too much for you?"

Petimus giggled. It was horrible.

"Mistress, I've done it," he said, attempting to divert the woman's attention onto his own achievements, like a jealous child.

The woman frowned and then motioned for the corpse to come inside. She set the bird's body upon the table. She muttered a few words.

"*Byť do tieňa,*" she said, having recited the incantation thousands of times, "*Aby mi slúžil mojím kolegom tieni.*" She looked at Petimus and Verdorben. "She's dead?"

"Your granddaughter is dead," Petimus announced triumphantly. Verdorben's ears perked up as the bird on the table began twitching and shedding feathers.

"Mm," Nalia grunted with approval. "I trust she was tasty?"

Petimus licked his teeth. If he had a properly functioning human stomach, it would certainly have growled. He looked at Verdorben and then at the ground, nervous.

"Ah...too skinny. No flesh. A few bites, but I prefer-"

"Spoiled wretch. Certain she's dead?"

Petimus hideously cowered next to the leg of the table, staring up at the woman with his bulging, snaky eyes.

"Certain, miss," he said, "not a breath left in her."

Verdorben growled as the crow on the table stood up and began slowly limping around, making weak and quiet squawks. Nalia started to gather up the feathers that it shed.

"Curious," she remarked, "that you did not take her into the shadows."

"Couldn't be seen, we were in the city."

"No matter, no matter, let her rot instead," the hag said as she placed the feathers in a bucket she kept under the table. "Only one is needed."

"One vessel of shadow?"

"One with me, the dark," the woman said. "Not a vessel of ice, that little abomination. Little blaspheming brat."

"Who then, shall it be? There's thousands, mistress."

"Not dead, like you. They are my people. Must be alive. A king. To rule beside me with my army of shadows. One worthy enough."

The woman watched as the bird started clamoring around the table, chasing the shadows of the flickering lantern that sat next to it. She smiled and took a deep breath as a haze filled her nostrils and a few wrinkles slowly vanished from her face.

"Further from my own mortal death. Shadows keep me young and well," she sighed, pleased with the element that restored her youth. She focused her attention back to her disgusting henchman."That little one. The lost boy, the special one. You fetch him. Find him," Nalia snapped, the black swimming furiously in her eyes. "Both of you, find him. Bring him. Make sure he isn't dead. Better not be dead. He escaped alive. Must be alive." Nalia stared at the floor intently as she muttered all of this.

"Where, miss?" Petimus asked. "That boy is long gone, he could be across the world."

"Start here. The treacherous city. Around the forest. The small towns. Must be alive. Must be here. I sense him. Sweet boy. Handsome boy. Dark. *Môj najsladší tieň.*"

Petimus tilted his head. Verdorben batted a paw at the now-flying, reanimated black crow. The woman seized her corpse-servant by the neck.

"Find him!"

Startled, Petimus shrank into the shadows, dragging his preoccupied hound with him to begin their next task.

Halvard and I sat next to each other at the large and otherwise empty table, watching as the kitchen maids brought dishes of food and laid them out on the table. The maids laid out the meal fit for royalty: roast venison, fluffy loaves of bread, and the freshest wines available. I looked at my brother, who had his pocket watch out.

"Somebody late?" I asked.

"Violet's been with Sullivan for almost fifteen minutes," my brother grumbled. "The boy is refusing to come to dinner."

"Pity," I said, helping myself to a glass of wine. "Your wife has finally come across someone who isn't afraid of her."

Halvard scowled at me, likely holding back the urge to land a blow on my smug face. He couldn't, now that we weren't children. Even still, he'd lose miserably against me in a brawl.

"I'm afraid he gets it from our side of the family," I said, after taking a thoughtful sip of the dry, rich red.

"From you, you mean."

"Where all of his best traits originated."

Seeing my brother's expression turn into such a painfully calm rage amused me greatly.

"Hardly."

"Miss Violet," the cook called merrily from the kitchen, "Beggin' your pardon, miss, but the soup is gettin' cold."

"Never mind the soup, Agatha," snapped a powerful voice. My sister-in-law stormed into the room, her corsetted hips swaying with her usual air of dominance. "We'll begin directly with the bread and venison tonight. Oh, don't bother with that, dear," she said as Halvard began to get up to pull a chair for his wife. He slowly sat back down. The black-haired woman yanked the chair from under the table and sat herself down, in a dignified huff. Looking at us, Violet noticed that each of us had raised eyebrows.

"Lizabet, a glass of wine," the woman ordered, ignoring our puzzled looks. The plump little maid nodded and poured Violet a glass.

"Your son," Violet began, addressing her husband, "Will not be joining us for dinner tonight, on his own accord," she said, her newly aging face cringing in displeasure. "Again."

Halvard slowly picked at a piece of bread.

"He must eat something," he mumbled.

"I wouldn't worry, he's young and bound to find food when he gets hungry," I noted. "Poor dear."

"This is the fourth night in a row, Shandar," Halvard snapped. "He'll eat on his own, but refuses to eat with us, with his own mother and father."

I shrugged and sipped my wine.

"Perhaps you treated him too harshly," I said.

"We forbade him from leaving this house until we feel we can trust him," Violet said, her cold glare focused directly on me. I couldn't look into her eyes without the fear of being turned to stone. "Though I fear that his influence is the one that should have been disciplined."

"I let him make his own decisions, you know," I said with a mouthful of venison. "And he chooses to come along with me."

"Just because he makes his own decisions does not mean they are advisable ones," Violet shot back. "All I ask is for there to be order in his life, and proper training on how to act as a young and civilized gentleman."

"He's acting just as young men do," my brother interjected. "Curious. Adventurous. But I'd rather not let my son be driven by obscene forces beyond his control."

I would have made a rude remark in response had I not looked up to see the couple glaring at me. I realized that the "obscene force" was myself.

"Perhaps you're jealous," I said, buttering a chunk of bread. "that I'm teaching him life lessons better than his own father."

I hadn't thought that quip through, though I often, by reflex or perhaps instinct, would say things that immensely upset my brother.

Halvard pursed his lips furiously and his cheeks grew red.

"I am at least trying to set a good example. I care for my son."

"And I don't?" I asked, my eyebrows going up. "At least I can make him happy."

"But not successful or intelligent!" Halvard said, his voice rising. "He must be taught how to be a respectable figure when I am gone!"

"It's done, as it seems I respect him and his decisions more than his own father."

Halvard sat there for a moment, before calling for a maid.

"A glass of wine, Lizabet," he said. "You must excuse me, darling, but I'm going to take a walk."

"Oh please dear, not you too!"

Before she could argue, Halvard had kissed his wife on the cheek and scurried off to take a long walk around the large and mostly empty house.

Halvard went into an empty room, a guest bedroom, and quietly shut the door. He set the wine down on the side table next to the bed, and sat down, putting his head in his hands. How dare his brother claim that he acts as a better father to Sullivan! How dare he encourage such vile and disgusting behavior! How dare he for being more charming and less grey than I!

I couldn't tell you precisely what my brother could have been brooding about, but this is the closest representation I can give you.

There was no doubt in his mind, however, that the oncoming headache had something to do with the horrible feeling of instinctual dread that crept into his mind. Like something leaked from the back of his brain and formed a puddle in the middle, clouding his thoughts further.

Distracting him from the situation he'd stormed away from. He brought a hand to his ear when he felt a tickle coming from it. He rubbed at it and pulled away, looking at his fingers. An inky black substance coated his fingertips. The man's heart sank to his stomach as the dread grew worse.

A slow knocking came at the door. Halvard jumped at the sound.

"Come in," he said, wrongfully expecting a familiar face such as myself or his wife.

The door opened, but nobody stood behind it. My brother creased his brow.

The wind? he thought, looking back to see if the window was open. When he turned towards the door again, two hideous creatures stood there, closing the door behind them.

A loud clattering filled the empty room as my brother gasped and knocked his glass from the side table. Through the dark, Halvard recognized the figures and felt an even deeper dread filling his stomach. "Petimus?"

"Best not to dirty your melodious voice with my name," the faintly glowing creature said. "We've missed you, little Halvard."

Halvard stared at the creature after not seeing it in years, not since he was a boy, lost and running through the snow. Dodging trees. Sobbing. He shook his head and swallowed his fear to the best of his ability. It didn't work very well, as he could hardly stand without trembling at the knees.

"'Tis no way to greet a fellow member of the shadow, ssskin-bag," Petimus replied, taunting the silent Halvard. "Buck up, boy."

"I hardly think inhuman creatures warrant a proper greeting," Halvard replied.

"Oh, how marvelously wretched, you've insulted me!" The creature appeared suddenly behind my brother from the shadows, causing Halvard to nearly trip over him backwards.

"What are you doing here?" Halvard hissed, flustered as anyone would be. Petimus gazed back without blinking his snaky eyes.

"Verdorben and I merely came to say hello," Petimus wheezed as he chortled with amusement at his own mischief. "After searching for you for days. Easy to find you. I see you've chosen to live so near to the woods. Good choice."

Verdorben snarled viciously at Halvard, baring his yellowed teeth and drooling black.

"To say hello," Halvard said with disbelief.

"I expected you to know why I'm here," Petimus replied, his voice more curt.

What a strange thing it is, to be in a state of both insatiable fear and terrible rage. Any outbursts of anger, when it came to Halvard, never ended well for him. The dripping black from his ear promptly reminded him of this. Therefore, he kept his emotions as controlled and collected as possible.

"Who sent you?"

Petimus let out a disgusting giggle.

"Who else?"

The veins in my Halvard's hand pulsed with flashes of black.

"Hasn't she done enough to me?"

"Done enough *for* you, you mean?"

Halvard rubbed at the bridge of his nose with his thumb and index finger, pressing into it in the hopes that the fear would vanish entirely. That *they* would vanish entirely.

"I'm refusing anything she asks of me, you tell her that. I'm not to be associated with her. Ever."

Verdorben gave Halvard a growl of disapproval.

"Nonetheless," Petimus said, "I shall relay the message from the great and noble, kind and caring sister of the shadow - Nalia."

Halvard wrinkled his brow at the sickeningly glorious address. Petimus smirked. He, unfortunately, couldn't do much else with his face.

"Nalia needs you, boy. She gave you gifts to use for her. She'll not be happy until she has you again."

Halvard wrenched his eyes away from the hideous thing.

"If I refuse?"

"You'll have to dig a grave of your own, then, boy."

"Your threats mean nothing to me."

"I suppose your trembling is due to the cold, then?" Petimus reached a bony hand to his companion and began stroking the beast. They sunk into the flickering shadows. Halvard felt that same warm trickle dripping from his ear to his neck. He fumbled with his inside pocket, feverishly looking for his handkerchief. A muffled voice came from the floor.

"The last of Nalia's family is dead. She's lost hope in her kin. They all betrayed her."

The flickering shadows erupted as Halvard swiped at the ground. An inky black puddle formed on the ground at his feet.

"Jura?" Halvard whispered.

"And Jura's bastard daughter, born of the cold and not of the shadow."

Petimus rose up from the floor, holding Halvard's deep blue handkerchief.

"Perhaps, if you'd like more time to consider, we'll be back to collect you for Nalia soon enough."

"That woman is mad. She couldn't have killed her own family!"

"Don't concern yourself with the dead past, boy," Petimus replied. "Perhaps she did, perhaps she didn't." Petimus licked his chops, recalling the feast he'd had that day, Jura's screams echoing in his sick mind. "Understand that she will not tolerate you being too late. Then we'll all be in deep trouble."

Petimus and Verdorben blended back into the shadows and disappeared completely, leaving no trace except the blue hanky. Halvard frantically searched the floor and the fire for signs of the two. Alas, the creatures were gone entirely now.

"Damn you!" he cried, hoisting himself up from the floor. "Petimus!"

Halvard stood in the empty room, waiting for that disgusting voice to come back. He sank into a chair after a tense few moments. Why would Nalia need him? No, why did she need him in the first place? She'd nearly killed him...or perhaps he'd nearly killed himself. The strain on his young body that day left him screaming in agony. The man fought back tears as he recalled the woman's old, bony fingers assaulting him, the hideous and inhuman screaming he'd done . . .

My brother noticed a small spider's web in the windowsill, with its resident alone with the remains of the past week's dinners. Halvard stared at the spider for a moment before he carefully placed his trembling finger to a thread of the web, allowing the black to pulse through his veins. A shadow oozed from his fingers until it dripped onto the web, turning the whole of the spider's home black within a second. The web collapsed as though it had been caught in a raging snowstorm.

Suddenly, Halvard's bowels churned violently. The entire encounter had turned him into a blithering, cowardly fool. And Jura was dead. Was it his own fault? The last of Nalia's kin, Petimus had said, were eradicated. Halvard stumbled out of the room, clutching his head and his abdomen, both of which pounded with pain.

Chapter 4

By far, one of the most dreaded places in all of Asterbury was the gloomy Charity Home for the Unfortunate. In other words, the workhouse, where many of the city's paupers lived in miserable harmony. The structure stretched around the corner of the city, where the poorest neighborhoods were constantly reminded of what might happen to their residents. Any of the city's paupers could end up in that wretched building that loomed over the city, like an uncomfortable shadow of guilt. I've known many a mother to warn their children to grow into hard workers, lest they become poor enough to be stuck there forever. It's too often described as something of an early hell.

The woman overseeing the girls' ward, a large and ungraceful Mrs. Evelyn Greensbury, held no charm, no elegance, and a repulsive sense of dominance over everyone she came across. Since the woman's nose was so often stuck in the air, she hardly noticed the ones below her, and treated them as such. Truly, the authorities chose the most nightmarish warden to watch over this prison.

Inside that large and terrible structure, the good doctor Howell, a man with a well-trained upright stature and perfectly tamed brown hair, stepped out of the relieving room with a sigh.

"I'm sorry, Mrs. Greensbury," he said, adjusting his round spectacles. "Whatever it was that attacked this girl frightened her into absolute silence, and now she refuses to speak. I imagine it was a wolf, judging by the wounds on her chest, arms and face. It's a miracle she's alive."

"How dreadful," was the unsympathetic reply from the simple-minded woman.

"However, the girl is indeed mobile," the doctor continued. "She's slow on her feet, but can otherwise hold her weight quite well, from what I've observed."

"Good scullery-maid, she'll make," Mrs. Greensbury thought aloud.

The doctor cleared his throat, sensing a squabble between the both of them.

"You must understand, Mrs. Greensbury, she must be given at least a few days to regain her strength," the doctor said. "The wounds will take time to heal. While they have been bandaged sufficiently, I cannot guarantee that she will be fit for working right away."

There was a moment of silence. You see, Doctor Howell was considered to be one of the kindest doctors in Asterbury. He spent much of his time in the workhouse, and made life more tolerable for its residents as the mistress had very little sense of compassion. Unfortunately, the horrible woman showed the doctor the same amount of sympathy as she did for anyone else, perhaps besides herself. Doctor Howell received a great deal of abuse from her, financially, to be specific. In this case, he was well aware that the cruel woman had every intention of putting the poor girl to work right away.

"When will she be able to work?" the woman asked, directly on cue.

"Likely in a fortnight."

Mrs. Greensbury glared at the kind and gentle face of the medical examiner, her own face representing that of a spoiled house cat. She let out a heavy sigh.

"No more than a fortnight," she growled. "If I may be so bold, Doctor Howell, you are not getting paid in your profession to be kind, rather to serve the Charity Home."

The doctor stood up straighter, though he never was the type of man to appear threatening.

"And if I may be so bold, Mrs. Greensbury, these girls are in need of some kindness, and I am to believe that they don't see any from you."

Knowing very well that he'd upset the woman, the doctor immediately returned to the relieving room, shutting the door behind him. He listened for the sound of heavy footsteps stomping away, then turned to face the girl seated on the examining table.

"Forgive me, miss, but it appears that the overseer has already determined where you will be working," he said. "Unfortunately, she's not one to change her mind very easily."

The brown-haired girl nodded as her gaze fell to the floor. She said nothing in reply.

"She agreed to allow a fortnight's worth of treatment for you, so that you're able to regain your strength and begin working in the kitchen as a scullery maid."

The girl nodded again. The doctor nervously cleared his throat as he lowered himself to be at eye level with her.

"Chin up, my dear," he said softly, lifting her head back up. "I understand this place and that woman are dreadful. But don't let it break your spirit." The doctor smiled his warmest smile. "I'll call the nurses to admit you into the sick ward. Wait here." Before he left, the doctor gathered up some papers. "It's required for us to know your name," he said. "Could you at least tell me what it is?"

The girl moved her large, sad eyes to the doctor.

"Romilla."

And so began the miserable life of Romilla in the Charity Home for the Unfortunate. They provided her with shabby clothing, a shabby bed, and short commons - so little nourishment that her healing was bound to be prolonged. Not two days had gone by when Mrs. Greensbury brought her into her office and stated that she was needed in the kitchen. As the doctor had predicted, she was not patient enough to let her recover for the full fortnight.

The kitchen, being loud and frightfully dirty, terrified Romilla. There were too many sounds of too many people bustling about and jostling each other around like fish in a net. Among the crowd of maids busying themselves, the girl would hear her name shouted.

"Romilla! Romilla!"

The constant shrill sound of the girl's name on the cook's lips barraged her ears from the morning to late at night, with no stopping. She ran up and down the stairs, in and out of the kitchen, back and forth. This happened for days on end, and the authorities sent her off to bed with nothing but a piece of bread, a slice of cheese, and a cup of water. Many of the other maids considered her the "fetching-girl", as she would be sent to the pantry to, as the title suggests, fetch things for the cooks. On one particular afternoon, Romilla, with her weakened muscles, dropped a large tray of dishes. They all shattered and scattered, creating a stunned silence from the other maids in the kitchen.

"You miserable little brat!" the cook screamed, as the other young girls all watched with a mixture of pity and amusement. "Mrs. Greensbury will hear about this display. Heaven help you then!"

"I-I'm sorry," the girl whispered. "I'm so sorry."

"After the missus is through with you, I'd imagine you certainly will be."

Very quickly after the incident, Mrs. Greensbury got word of this and gave the girl a blow to her ear when they were alone. Romilla crumpled to the ground, tears streaming down her face, yet no sobs emerged from her lips.

"Native klutz!" the woman scolded, giving the girl another blow. "Frost-creeper! Those were our best dishes! How are we to serve our guests now?!"

Poor Romilla cried. She couldn't have possibly realized it, but the terrible woman had lied; no guests would visit such a place. One fascinating trait that Mrs. Greensbury had about her, though also extremely cruel, was a sort of creative side. She often found herself coming up with a great amount of insults and names that no one else heard except for inside the Charity Home. She fancied herself a sort of poet in this regard, though a new name never bode well for any of the girls afflicted with it.

It was from this point on that poor Romilla was no longer referred to by her name, but by "frost-creeper". Now,

Mrs. Greensbury came up with this degrading title because of the girl's native descent. However, in many cases, the girl walked into a room full of people and saw each of them step away from her, rubbing their arms or shuddering. The girls' gossip began to spread that Romilla herself would bring a curious chill into the room, not by opening windows, but simply by being there, and especially when she cried.

When he arrived at the workhouse, the doctor went into the relieving room, where most of his examinations were carried out. Doctor Howell flipped through his notes full of important dates. He looked at the date for that day: January 24th. A name was scrawled on his messy agenda page: *Romilla*. He asked for one of the girls to fetch Romilla, who soon appeared in the room, dressed in a long, patched-up tunic and nervously wringing her hands. After a quick look at the claw wounds on her belly, arms, and face, Doctor Howell treated the ones that were healing slower. While doing so, he attempted to strike up a friendly conversation with the girl to put her more at ease.

"I have to say you're duly better than you were when I first took you in," he remarked. "Has Mrs. Greensbury been good to you?"

Romilla hesitated before speaking.

"Yes, sir."

Doctor Howell knew what a truth that was-in short, it wasn't.

"Now, don't feel the need to lie, young lady," the doctor said in a lower voice. "Tell me the truth; how have they been treating you?"

Romilla didn't reply. She only looked down.

"That's precisely what I was afraid of," Doctor Howell mumbled. Of course, they'd been ghastly to her. That's what happened to every single soul admitted into that building. Why should it have been any different with

Romilla? Surely, because she came in so injured, they would have thought it wise to actually help her. No, not here. The doctor silently fumed over these musings. "Please tell me what she's done," he said at last, regaining composure.

Romilla's brown eyes darted around the room, as if she felt the walls were listening. The doctor noted just how the question suddenly gave her a case of nerves. He'd seen it all too often, the girls would scramble to find a suitable lie to save them from future punishment.

"I can't," she answered simply.

"Romilla."

The way that the doctor made his voice more stern caused the girl to tense up. She backed away as if he had just threatened her.

"I won't hurt you, Romilla," he reassured her, puzzled. "I promise you."

Doctor Howell thought he felt a gust of cold wind. He looked at the window, wondering if it was open.

Romilla never answered the question. Her bottom lip quivered. The doctor rubbed his right arm with his left hand. The chill seemed more noticeable now.

"Romilla?"

Still no answer. The windows weren't even open, how could the wind be coming through nonetheless?

"This must be the coldest room in the establishment," the doctor muttered, trying to find the source of the draft. When he looked back at Romilla, she was playing nervously with her braided hair.

"Cold, sir?" she asked timidly.

"Have you not noticed the cold?"

Romilla shook her head immediately.

"No, sir. I've not."

A low growl suddenly came from the girl's stomach. The doctor shook his head.

"Have they given you a speck of food?" he asked.

The girl stared even more intently at the floor.

The righteous man lost his temper now, frustrated

that he had his answer.

"I told that woman to let you alone for a fortnight, and she's already been miserably treating you," the man mumbled angrily. "Dressed in rags and underfed, she knows you were horribly battered, and yet she still refuses to listen. Better conditions out on the streets!"

Romilla stood there, quietly sniffling. The doctor looked back at her. Poor, sweet, quiet Romilla. Brought into civilization just to be abused.

"Oh dear, I'm sorry for frightening you," the doctor said, pulling a hanky from his pocket and giving it to the girl. She looked at it curiously. The doctor frowned. "Wipe your eyes, and your nose," he said.

This sort of behavior and interaction between the doctor and the girls in the workhouse was, of course, nothing new. He'd had this conversation with many of the girls, but no situation had thrown off the man's patience like that of Romilla's. How would you feel if you had to watch hundreds of young girls starving to death in such a miserable pile of rock?

The doctor's overwhelming compassion gave him an idea. This sort of idea may very well have put his own life and reputation in danger. His impulse, however, didn't come from worrying about his own life, but rather about that of others. Of Romilla's.

"How would you like to leave this place?"

Romilla's eyes widened, not with wonder, but with fear. She shook her head.

"Oh, no, Doctor," she answered, her eyes red and puffy. "I could never-I couldn't...I could hardly leave."

"I could find you work. With a proper home and proper money, you could live such a full life."

"She's hardly started here, Doctor Howell."

The large, painted Mrs. Greensbury stepped into the room, towering over the girl. Romilla put her face in her hands as the woman's hands gripped her shoulders tightly.

"Might I discuss this matter with you in private,

then, Mrs. Greensbury?" the doctor inquired, his hatred for the woman causing his chest to tighten.

"She's got a job of her own, Doctor, and she only just said she'd like to stay. And now you're planning on taking her away from me?"

"What has she eaten, Mrs. Greensbury?"

The big woman scoffed, her puffed chest causing her pearls to rattle.

"That's not my concern in this establishment, that's for the cooks to decide. If the girls are ill-mannered, they will not eat until they've learned to behave."

"That's a wretched way of treating these girls, and you especially can't tend to the injured like that!"

"May I remind you that you, Mortimer, were the one that decided upon bringing her to me?"

"I knew the moment she stepped foot in this building that my decision was a poor one," the doctor replied, slamming his papers down on the table. "No one should be allowed in such a treacherous place, where the only caretakers they know do nothing but treat them like rubbish! *Rubbish*, Evelyn!"

"This is the way things are, doctor," Mrs. Greensbury said, her own face turning pink, "And you know full well I have the law on my side." She yanked Romilla to the side by her arm. The girl cried in pain and cowered against the wall, terrified for the doctor. "If you can't be bothered with *my* manner of going about *my* business, then I'd suggest you bite your tongue and leave without another word! God help you when Asterbury paints you as such rabble!"

The doctor's bold righteousness overwhelmed him. He stood in front of the woman, like a brave knight in front of a dragon.

I'll warn you, my friends, to never trifle with a stout-hearted man.

"Very well, Mrs. Greensbury. I refuse to tolerate such misconduct towards your tenants, and furthermore I hereby renounce my position as head doctor in this Charity Home. I will find new, better homes for them, so that they won't be submitted to your disgusting treatment."

"You miserable blackguard!" the woman blurted, nearly reaching out and grabbing the doctor. "You incessant quack! You have no right! I'll lose my business!"

"This is no business, but hell! I have every right to help give these girls a future! Good day to you, and good riddance!"

Once the woman had stormed out of the relieving room, the doctor angrily regathered his papers. Enough was enough. He looked at Romilla, who, along with every other girl in the corridor, stared back at him, stunned. Romilla's eyes contained the sincere gratitude of a lost puppy returned to its owner. The doctor whispered to her.

"I can't stand by and let this woman mistreat everyone ," he admitted. "I'll find somewhere for you, you'll see." He turned to the other poorly dressed girls in the hall. "For all of you."

As he left, the doctor fanned himself with his papers. Sweat built up on his forehead. What a task that awaited him now.

"*Day 12, and I'm still alive. The Reditum has yet to consume my body and spirit,* " came a mumbling voice from a man in a handmade fur coat.

A distant cry from a wolf sounded, as if on cue. The man tightly wrapped his hands around his last loaf of bread. He scribbled in his journal.

"*No sign of edible wildlife,*" he noted. "*Food rations are low.*"

The noble explorer ate half of his bread and continued forward. The sky grew darker with the heavy gray winter clouds. Nevertheless, the man pressed on.

"Such nonsense, these tales of ghosts and witches,"

he said, tossing aside a small purple book, the book that had inspired him to traverse into the cold and unforgiving labyrinth of the Reditum forest. His words dissolved in front of his reddened face, in a cold cloud. Reassuring oneself day after day can grow tiring, after all. It's best to accept things as they are, and as they come. Some, like this man, are far too proud to accept this fact.

  The man sniffed at the air. The smell of smoke wafted into his nostrils. A fire, this deep in the woods? Surely he wasn't imagining things?

  "Is...is someone there?"

  There, in a small clearing, sat a wooden hut with a smoldering fire in front of it. Flickering lights shone through the two windows, barely visible through the snowfall. He stepped towards the cabin, but stopped as he reached the door.

  "No, no, I have to press on," he told himself. "Musn't bother whomever's home."

  As he started to walk away, a gust of wind whipped at his face, causing his already teary eyes to water even more.

  "Maybe just a knock," he mumbled.

  The door swung open, nearly hitting the explorer.

  "No need," came an old voice from behind the door. The explorer, being rather tall, looked down to see an old woman clad in a cloak made out of wolf pelt and adorned with black and brown feathers. She appeared both regal and humble, for an old woman living in the forest. Her hair was wild and gray, and her face appeared to have concealed wrinkles. Her fingernails were as black as the feathers she wore.

  "I do apologize," the man stammered. "If I'm intruding."

  "No need," the woman repeated. "Must be cold, hm?"

  The man sniffled a nose dripping back into his nostril.

"Y-yes, ma'am."

"Come in, come in."

The explorer stepped into the strange cabin. It wasn't very big, and didn't seem to have much space for him. He needed to crouch to avoid much of the ornamental decorations hanging from the ceilings. They seemed to be trinkets from all over the world-compasses, brooches, jewelry, and all manner of shiny things. The woman carried a tray with two wooden cups to the man.

"Fresh tea?"

The man seated himself on a cushioned stool, which creaked as he lowered himself into it. He graciously accepted the cup and began to sip at it. He couldn't recognize the flavor.

"Umbraberry leaves," the woman said. "Good and strong."

The man simply nodded. After he'd taken a few sips of the bitter tea, he winced and cleared his throat.

"Exploring the Reditum?" the woman asked.

"Ah, yes. I'm going to make it to the other end," he explained, his pride taking over again. "It hasn't been easy, but I will do it."

The woman let out a giggle.

"Nobody survives," she said. "How do you expect to?"

The man picked up the slightest trace of an accent in her voice. He couldn't identify it.

"I..." his voice faded out. He'd just run out of food, and he couldn't tell where in the forest he was. So answering the old hag's question in the moment was, undoubtedly, impossible.

"Best rest," she mumbled. "Dream of the answer."

"Oh, but...I don't mean to intrude-"

"Nonsense. It's cold. Windy. Snowy. Must regain your strength."

The woman motioned to the tiny cot on the floor in the corner. The man hesitated, but he laid down on the cot.

She pulled a blanket over him.

"Name?" she asked.

"Edward," the man replied. "What can I call you?"

The woman smiled as the tea leaves started to dissolve the wooden cup.

"Nalia," she answered. "Sleep, boy."

Almost immediately, the man slipped into a deep sleep. Nalia looked on as he started to snore, and then slowly but surely, the snoring came to a stop as his chest sank and never rose again. She put her wrinkled hand on his chest. His heart stopped beating entirely. The light from her fire started fading, followed by a hissing as though it had gone out.

"Another soul for the shadows," came the snaky voice. "Well done, milady."

Nalia reached behind her, not watching, and touched the corpse-creature's head like he was an obedient pet. Verdorben stood next to the corpse, walking in a circle until he laid down.

"Nobody survives," she said.

Petimus nodded.

"I should mention, milady, the news."

"News?" she asked, stirring up her own cup of tea and taking a sip. "What of, the precious vessel? The dear boy?"

"Young Master Halvard refuses to cooperate. Although, he's not young anymore. Quite old."

"Bad news," Nalia muttered. "We'll make him cooperate."

"Yes, yes, my lady," the thing stuttered.

"You show me him. Bring him to me. I gave him gifts. Did he not understand to use them for me?"

"He ran away years ago, so I would wager that means he didn't want to."

"How dare you!" the woman snapped. "How dare him! I sacrificed myself for that brat!"

"You burnt him," Petimus replied, cowering under the woman's enraged eyes. "He called it a curse."

Nalia kicked over a stool in a sudden violent rage, not unusual for her. Verdorben jumped up and whimpered, cowering next to Petimus.

"He knows. He must know. I'll tell him. I'll rip him from his home! No, you will! Take him from what he loves! I need that boy, he shall lead my people! He will lead my people!"

"Y-yes, Nalia," Petimus stammered, backing into the wall as the hag threw miscellaneous objects at the ground, some shattering, others falling with a heavy clunk. She stopped for a moment to plaster a smile across her face.

"Better yet," the woman crooned, suddenly sweet and charming, "Take what he loves from him first. Do not return until you've convinced him to come to me."

As she was about to retire to her room, Petimus stopped her.

"What about the sleeping explorer?" He pointed to the newly dead body in the corner. Nalia smirked and stomped the floor once. A black mass traveled from her foot's place in the floor to the cot. The body began to turn gray and bony as any remaining sign of life drained from it.

"*Byť do tieňa, aby mi slúžil mojím kolegom tieni.*"

The veins in the fresh corpse filled with black. His eyes snapped open, no longer colored, or human.

"Let him into the woods," Nalia ordered her oldest companion. "He'll make a hearty and sturdy soldier, don't you agree?"

The witch disappeared behind her curtain as Petimus led the clumsy, teetering corpse outside.

Chapter 5

"The photographer is here, Sullivan!"

I sipped at my wine as Violet went to fetch her son. Halvard made dull and idle conversation with the stocky man. We were now waiting for the star of the night to come downstairs and sit still for roughly an hour.

"Ah, don't you remember the days when mother made us sit for portraits?" I asked my brother as he walked over to me. "Hours on end, while we made remarks about the painter?"

"Ancient history," Halvard replied. "We've made advances since then, Sullivan should feel lucky."

He should have, but the boy sulked down the stairs as if he were being led to a postmortem photo instead. Perky, dirty blond hair tied in the back, a plain red vest paired with a black shirt, and a lovely pair of silk trousers, all walked into the living-room, carrying the height of misery along with them. Sullivan's youthful, stubbly face changed as he greeted the photographer - he smiled. It was an act, the dignified and polite way he spoke. He looked at me, and I smirked back at him.

"Come to watch the festivities, uncle?" he asked.

"Rather, to advise," I replied. "Keep a cheeky look on your face, it will look far better on the walls."

Sullivan narrowed his eyes at my advice.

"You know you came to laugh at me."

I put my hand under my chin and looked up at the ceiling.

"Hmm...all right, so I have. You've caught me."

"Let's get this over with quickly," Violet said, her hand on the boy's shoulder. "And please do not distract the boy, Shandar," she said under her breath.

"As you wish, milay," I said, taking another sip.

And with that, the photo commenced. It did take quite a while, and Sullivan's mother and father stood behind the photographer for the entirety of the time, as a stern reminder for him to look as regal as possible. I sat in an armchair, reading through a small book of poetry and studying the flow of the words, occasionally glancing up and smirking at my nephew. I wondered how some of those words of poetry would sound to a beautiful woman if I rehearsed and recited them to her. It was like a serenade, but I'm certainly no cantor.

"Finally," I heard the young and relieved voice say as it approached me. Sullivan pulled his hair out of its confines and back to its shoulder-length glory. "Felt as though it would never end."

"All good things must come to an end, my boy," I said, laying wisdom before him like a good uncle should. "Getting a perfectly lifelike image of yourself is something you should be happy about."

"Too bad it's dull," the boy said. "I would much rather be in a pub, speaking with-"

I cleared my throat as a warning while the boy spoke. Halvard stood directly behind his son.

"I was going to thank you, Sullivan, for sitting nicely, but now I'm curious."

I chuckled.

"As am I," I said.

"-speaking with my uncle," the boy finished, turning to glower at his father. "I enjoy speaking with my uncle."

"Hm," Halvard grunted before stepping away to pay the photographer.

Sullivan began walking away, then turned to me, expecting me to follow. I did.

"What's on your mind, boy?" I asked. "Your mother and father have been worried sick about you for days. Have you anything to say for yourself?"

The boy let out a long sigh.

"I'm tired of them," he said. "I'm tired of them and their lessons and their 'proper' lifestyles. I want to be more like you. I can't seem to have that with them around."

I nodded, because I was the very same as a boy. My

own mother favored Halvard for his responsible behaviors and mannerisms. I could understand my nephew quite well, he'd been thrown into the very same situation as I. And now look at me, borrowing my brother's wealth. I didn't want that for the boy. He didn't have any brothers or sisters to borrow from. Though inheriting his father's wealth was the most likely possibility. So really, what did he have to worry about?

"Uncle?"

I snapped out of my daze.

"You are a boy," I said. "And boys shall learn these things in due time. Someday you'll come to thank your father for his efforts. It's something you must grow out of."

"I am grown."

"No, no you aren't," I answered dryly. "Not in the eyes of your father and mother. Nor I. You're still young."

"And you believe you're better, I suppose?" he retorted, stopping in his tracks. "Better than I am, because of your age."

"My boy, I said nothing of the sort-"

"I don't think you understand how low they think of you, uncle. They gossip about you. Talking of your scandalous affairs and your influence on me. They say you're nothing but a burden on this family."

"I can handle the critique, boy," I said with a sharp tone of voice. Perhaps I couldn't. "Listen to me, people are all different. Just because we come from the same family does not mean that you have to be like your father. You are Master Sullivan Vrana. You're young. And handsome. And perhaps mischievous. But, another thing that you are not is me. You are not your father, your mother, nor your uncle."

Sullivan paused, possibly feeling bad about the outburst.

"I'd rather live the life you lead, uncle, than them. It's...it's loads of fun."

"Then consider the consequences."

"What consequences?" he scoffed. "Living the high

life of luxury, kissing as many women as I want, feeling them, gathering wealth for good food and drink and fine clothes?"

"Not in the slightest, Sullivan," I said, turning on my heels. "My own family despises me."

Not wanting to admit upset, I downed the rest of my wine and sauntered away from the boy. He was right - his mother and father did truly seem to hate me. But what did I care? Why should I worry? Maybe I should listen to my own advice. I am myself, I should not be concerned. And yet, for some reason, I was.

☙

Halvard finished speaking to the photographer and saw him out with a firm farewell. Violet left to continue work through the house, getting ready for supper, while my brother stood there, completely and utterly stunned. Something left him immobile. Dread pooled in the middle of his mind again, taking over whatever thoughts he had previously. *Drip, drip, drip*, he heard - rather, he thought he heard. A slight fizzling tickled at his right ear. Sensing the inevitable, he opened his ornate vest to pull the hanky from it. He dabbed at his ear with the lacy cloth. Pulling it away revealed that sticky, inky black substance.

How could this return to me? he asked himself. After all, everything that he'd done in past years since that day were efforts to control it. To never make the curse see the light of day again. And of all times, now! When his son needed to be tended to most of the time. Monitored, watched, while he was under the care of his devious uncle. Of course, now, when it had been so controlled, so meticulously taken care of. And now, it resurfaced. It brought back the screams of himself, the eyes of the girl that saved him, and the horrid blackened hands of the witch who'd brought this upon him.

Halvard realized that a few of his maids were staring, wondering whether or not to say a word to him. He cleared his throat and hastily put away the hanky.

"Apologies," he said, "I've been lost in thought."

My brother soon saw that one maid's eyes were reddened with tears.

"What's the matter?" Halvard asked.

Violet ran up behind the girl, breathless.

"Lizabet," the maid said, her voice shaking, "I found her covered in blood inside the library."

The girl could barely say that last bit without bursting into tears. A horrified shock rose in Halvard's chest. He began giving orders, his voice strangely calm.

"Violet, tell the maids in the kitchen to find safety- they must lock every door, seal themselves in whatever room they stand in. I fear there's an intruder."

"Yes, darling. I'll fetch Sullivan and your brother as well."

"Please be safe."

She scurried in the opposite direction, lifting her skirts up slightly to hurry away. "We need to act," Halvard said to the crying maid. "Gather up some of the young men. Check these rooms and shut all of the doors."

"What about the police?" the girl asked.

"We can send someone to notify them, though it may be too late," my brother explained. "We must act now."

⚘

Halvard started shutting doors haphazardly, hardly paying attention to where he was in his own home. Something in the back of his mind alerted him that the intruder may not have been a normal one. Something, of course, meaning the trickle of black that he could feel bubbling from the inside of his head earlier. When he reached the library, he noticed a few dark red drops leading into it. He opened the door.

"Lizabet, are you in here?"

No answer followed. Halvard ran his shoe across one drop of blood-it smeared the floor, still nearly fresh. A sheer, blind curiosity urged my brother to step inside, wherever the trail of blood drops led him. He crept into the library, his heart beating mercilessly inside his chest. He knew he was the only one armed to put up a proper fight and likely win. That, it seemed, is what the trickle of black liquid now against his neck told him.

The blood drops spread alongside the shelves, weaving in and out with them. They were smudged in places, evenly spaced in others, splattered and dribbled in others, and abruptly stopped at the wall. Halvard's breath heaved as he frantically searched for more blood drops, the source of the blood, for anything. He had trapped himself in the corner of the room, between the volumes of dark poetry and the history of Skadi, our homeland. Halvard's favorite as a child. One he hadn't visited since his youth. A portion of the room so forgotten that dust caked each shelf, each book, even the ground.

"Where are you?" he whispered. "Lizabet?"

"Master..."

The young girl's voice came from overhead. Startled, my brother watched as fresher, warmer blood dripped from the top of the shelves.

"Lizabet!"

The girl, sprawled belly-down across the top of the shelves and dripping dark blood onto the floor, pointed to the flickering candles on the wall. Her eyes were wide with stunned terror.

"Sh-shadows," she stuttered. "Master, the shadows."

Halvard tried his very best to completely disregard the obvious, but the witness voiced a truth that rang loud and clear. He merely brushed it off, though the dread, the terrible, awful sense of dread taunted his thoughts.

"Shadows...L-Liz, I'll get you down. We'll call a doctor."

Halvard yanked stacks of books onto the floor to clear room for him to climb up. The large, small, heavy and colorful pocket-books all tumbled to the ground without care. The maid shook her head vigorously as her master stepped to the first shelf.

"Master, they'll kill you. They'll kill me. They'll kill anyone."

No, don't let it be, Halvard thought. He would have preferred a human perpetrator than the ones that the maid spoke of. If his senses were correct.

"Don't worry-I'm here now, I'll get you out of here, you will be fine."

Halvard crawled up the shelves like a ladder, shaking as he wondered if they would hold his weight. When he reached the top, his face fell at the sight of her-bloodied chest, legs, and arms, all pooling and dripping down the numerous books filling the shelves. Horrific. He resisted the urge to gag.

"Can you move, Lizabet?"

The maid shook her head.

Tottering slightly, he turned around so that his back faced the girl, slid one arm under her belly, and shuffled her forward until she rested across his shoulders. Struggling, being the gaunt man that he was, Halvard managed to cautiously carry the girl all the way down from the shelves.

"Put me down, master," she whispered as he got to the floor. "Please. Don't let them get you."

"Nonsense, everything will be fine. Don't talk like that."

Halvard's chest tightened with every false reassurance he gave himself. The killer had only left this victim partially dead, like it was a game. A tricky character.

From the darkest corner of the room came a gruesome recital.

"Beware the beggar, little one."

Halvard's heart dropped into his stomach. He recognized those lines. He set the girl across the sofa in front of the hearth.

"No, no, it isn't true," he stammered.

"... *look away, little one, don't give in to his plea.*"

Halvard stood over the girl, looking all around the room for the source.

"*Alas, it's too late, your young mind is now ruined.*"

The fire roared and crackled. Halvard held up his arms in a flimsy attempt to protect the girl.

"*You've caught his golden green eyes.*"

"Enough of those horrid lines, you repulsive creature!" Halvard screamed.

Startled out of her shock, the girl snapped back into reality and let out a wail. She sat up and threw her hands around Halvard, desperate for a source of security.

"I don't want to die, master! I don't want to die!" Halvard watched as the fireplace began to dance, and collapse, and dance again. Two shadows oozed from inside and onto the floor in front of it. Lizabet's eyes caught the floor. "No, no!" she screeched, forcing herself into the cushions of the sofa, thus pushing it back. "Stay away!"

"Lizabet, run! Go to the-"

"I can't! I can't!"

With her cries of terror, Petimus and Verdorben rose from the ground, both seeping with extreme black from the nooks and crannies of their deformed bodies.

"Why Halvard, have you come to join us in our feast?" Petimus hissed.

The man inched towards the thing bravely, his arms still outstretched to protect the maid. His voice shook when he spoke.

"How dare you torment my servants, you disgusting creature."

Black liquid dripped from Halvard's ear onto the ground. He ignored it.

"I warned you," Petimus replied with what could only be described as a chuckle. "She's a good, plump little one. And me poor pup and I are starving near to death.

Would have gotten away quietly if not for your other little brats."

"You stay away from her," Halvard said, noticing his hands shook as much as his voice. "Leave my house, I'm warning you now."

Petimus waved a bony arm at him.

"Do not trifle with hungry beasts, Master Halvard."

When the corpse clicked his tongue, Verdorben lunged for the screaming, begging girl, taking her skirts in his powerful jaws.

"Master!" she screamed. "Master, help me!"

Halvard slammed his fist into the floor, as if it were instinct. A shadow rushed from his arm and into both of the creatures' bodies. Petimus yelped in pain. Verdorben's body twitched. Halvard gestured to the shadows from the fireplace. He formed them into a long strand that never left the ground, and used the strand to pull both creatures' feet together. When they tripped, Halvard did his best to pick up the immobile girl. He weaved through the bookshelves to reach the exit.

Petimus shot up from the ground in front of them. The man stumbled backwards, and the maid fell on top of him. Petimus grabbed her by the legs with both bony arms, waiting for Verdorben to appear by his side.

"I must thank the host for such a delightfully exciting meal," Petimus wheezed, having no trouble holding the struggling girl around his hunched, bony back. "Quite thrilling to catch food on the go, you know. But do not forget the words of Nalia, we shall return again soon, for you, burnt man."

Before Halvard could attempt any sort of resistance, Petimus and Verdorben dragged the girl back into the fireplace, where she let out an ear-piercing shriek. Stunned and shocked, Halvard realized the gravity of what he'd just witnessed. A sick nausea rose in his gut as he thought of what the creatures were going to do to his maid.

"No! Lizabet! Petimus, stop! Please!"

Halvard banged his fists on the mantle, as the fire continued to roar. He could hardly follow the murderers into the fire. He stopped and looked at the sofa, breathing heavily. Fresh blood smeared the upholstery and the floor.

Halvard knelt in front of the fireplace, his tears stinging his eyes as much as the heat from the fire. He let out a roar of agony.

What had he done?

Chapter 6

Lizabet was dead. That is what Halvard told the household.

"There was...blood everywhere," he said, struggling to describe the situation without a tremble in his voice. "I can't imagine she survived whatever attack it was."

A plethora of detectives and law authorities came and went over the week of mourning, all attempting and failing to find any evidence that might lead to the killer.

"Not more than a month ago, we documented a similar attack on the streets of the city," one of the pompous detectives informed my brother. "If this is the same attacker, it's curious that he would strike directly in your home, and at a maid no less."

Not one of the officials could find the source of the death, or even find out if the girl had been taken somewhere else. I didn't wish to participate in the activity, myself, however. Being a bystander in both of the most recent murder mysteries toyed with my mind. When I found myself lost in thought, usually thinking back to that girl in the street, I drowned out the loud thoughts with sherry or gin, or whatever else I could get my hands on. Soon, I stopped drinking it at my brother's house and found myself sauntering off to the city alone, looking for a scandalous woman to make me forget everything temporarily.

The rest of the household, from what I'd gathered, reacted similarly. Halvard spent many hours locked in a room, sometimes heard shouting. Violet shed some tears, but continued to run the household, though now more irritable and liable to lash out at any servant who, affected by the same tragedy, slipped up.

As for my nephew, I would have offered to bring him into the city with me, but I never thought of it in my own constant, mindless, and drunken state. He acted similarly to his father, except he quietly spent hours upon hours in the library. The boy looked aimlessly up and down the shelves, passing by a few maids scrubbing at dark stains on the light, dusty hardwood in the very corner. One of them looked up at her young master and shook her head.

"Ah, Master Sullivan, there's no reason for you to be here," she said, tears pooling in her eyes. "Surely this is a gruesome sight to see."

"I'm not fazed much, Isabelle," the boy replied, both fascinated and repulsed by the sight of the maids cleaning up the dried blood of their own colleague.

"Aye, but to mourn one that died far too soon," Isabelle said, pulling a small purple book from the large pile or books on the ground, "could break a child's heart, it could."

"I'm no child anymore," Sullivan said, though not with bitterness.

"Begging your pardon, Master Sullivan," Isabelle sighed, looking at the little purple leather-bound volume. "You're a child in my eyes, still young and sweet."

Sullivan crouched to Isabelle on the ground to get a better look at that little book. The title, though faded, read, *An Incomplete Compendium of the Reditum.*

"May I?" he asked.

Isabelle handed it to him. The boy flipped through each yellowed page, noting both the neatly printed text and the scrawled handwriting throughout.

"Goes with the small pocket-volumes," Isabelle said, pointing in the direction of the shelf.

"I'll put it away for you," Sullivan said, intrigued by the tiny little thing.

"Many thanks, lad," Isabelle said, an exhausted gratitude filling her voice.

Sullivan left the scene of the crime. He looked back to see if anyone was in sight. When he saw no one, the boy left the library, stuffing the little book into his inside pocket.

My brother didn't invite too many people to the funeral, as he didn't want to create a large stir. I would say it was a lovely ceremony, had Lizabet not died at the hands of a brutal killer. The maid's family, some of Halvard's university friends, Doctor Mortimer Howell (and a girl he had taken in, I discovered as they arrived), and the entirety of our household attended the ceremony that day. Everyone shivered in the cold while the memorial commenced and the church official read the last rites for the girl. Every now and again I would look back at the small crowd. It was an interesting sight to see, the sea of black clothes against the white snow.

Once the last rites were spoken, the crowd dispersed and mingled. I walked with Sullivan through the grounds of the cemetery, both of us puffing on cigarettes to ease the grief. We didn't speak a word to each other as we walked.

"Mr. and Mrs. Vrana, I'm deeply sorry for your loss," the young Doctor Howell said as he approached Halvard and Violet.

"Thank you, doctor," my brother replied. "It was kind of you and your guest to attend."

The young thing looked at Halvard with large eyes. Notably, the structure of her face was foreign to anyone who lived in or around the city, and two long scars ran across it. No one who looked at her could ignore the striking pale streaks against the slightly darker face.

"Ah, this is Romilla," the doctor said, bringing the quiet girl forward. "Romilla, this is Mister Halvard Vrana. I've been looking after the poor girl since the Charity Home treated her so terribly. She's no parents or family around, poor thing."

"None at all?" Violet asked, the tears still fresh in her eyes from the mourning.

"Unfortunately not," the doctor said. "A good home will do her well, I think, after all she's been through."

"I'm sure," Halvard replied.

"Oh, oh," Violet uttered as she noticed the girl's lips

quivering and tear droplets falling down her cheeks. "No need to cry, dear." She wiped the tears from the girl's eyes with a lacy hanky.

"Yes, she's very prone to these tears," Doctor Howell explained, leaning closer to Halvard. "Many a family has turned her down due to her constant tears."

"Rubbish," Violet said. "Absolute rubbish. Does no one see that she needs a good home? Halvard, why not take her in as a maid? After all, we need one."

Her husband looked at her with mild shock. The woman was emotional, for certain, but this seemed too sudden, especially for her. He attempted to put forward some logic.

"Now, Violet, we might want to discuss this further later, this isn't the right time. You're emotionally torn, we must talk when you aren't."

"Oh, please, dear, the poor thing has no one," the woman said. "Wouldn't you like a family to stay with if your own left you?"

"I...well, I suppose. But we should discuss the living arrangements, and the work she can do."

"She's a strong worker, eager to learn," the doctor chimed in. Halvard didn't appear amused that the doctor seemed to be agreeing with the sudden ideas of his wife.

"Why not let her speak for herself?" Violet interjected. "Romilla, dear, how would you like to stay with us and work for us?"

The girl looked at the doctor, looked at Violet, and then looked at Halvard. To her surprise, Halvard suddenly stared at her, his eyes blazing with an intense emotion that she could not recognize.

"Romilla, would you like to stay with and work for the Vranas?" the doctor asked. "This is a wonderful family, well-renowned and very clearly fond of each and every person in their household."

The girl whispered into the doctor's ear. He nodded, then straightened up.

"She agrees," he confirmed. "We will go back to my house and gather up her things. Mister and Mrs. Vrana, I cannot thank you enough for your compassion. Tomorrow, she will be ready for work."

After bidding the guests goodbye and sending them off, Halvard took one last look at Romilla, the girl with the scars. He couldn't help but find her native features terribly familiar.

∽∮∾

The next week or so following that somber ceremony proved to be a dull one. I hadn't much to do while the rest of the household mourned for the lost maid. Everyone worked slower, some needed time away, and so on. One particular day, I'd woken up from a fitful sleep to the sound of knocking.

"Mmm?" I replied, both arms draped miserably over my face. I heard the door open. It surprised me to see Halvard at my door whilst I lay in bed, moping.

"Shandar, I need a favor from you today."

Ah, lovely. He had a task for me to carry out. I didn't move.

"You require help from the ever-celebrated prodigal son?" I mumbled.

"No, I need help from you."

Fair enough.

"What do you need from me?" I asked.

"I'm going to need you to come into the city with me," Halvard replied. I removed the arm that covered my eyes. He was already dressed to go out. "We are escorting a new maid to the house. I believe having the both of us would be beneficial, seeing as she's quite nervous and shy. Not to mention needs safety in light of recent events."

I chuckled, bitter from the entire mourning process. I put my arm back.

"That didn't take very long, did it?"

"Ultimately, it was Violet's choice," Halvard said. "We spoke with the girl and Doctor Howell at Lizabet's memorial, and then talked it over amongst ourselves. Doctor Howell said she was in need of a home, and Violet couldn't help her motherly instincts."

I dragged my arms away from my face specifically to exchange glances with my brother. It was a knowing look, one that said, 'Violet has made up her mind and will not change it under any circumstance'. Both of us were absolutely aware of this. I sat up.

"I suppose I'd be more than happy to do something other than mill about the castle."

My brother's face twisted with slight displeasure. He never appreciated my use of the word "castle" to describe their home.

"Perhaps this was not a good idea," he mumbled loud enough for me to hear, his fingers massaging his pale temples. He got up from his chair and handed off a piece of paper to one of the maids. "We leave in no more than an hour. Be ready, and, for the love of all that is holy, be civil."

When we arrived in Asterbury, the streets were bustling with people, going in and out of their respective workplaces and wandering through the market. The buildings looked promising, homey, and comfortable. Children ran through the streets, playing and chasing each other. The men and women dressed nicely, though perhaps not as nicely as my brother and I, who wore long, thick cloaks and silk hats. The bright snow dotted our fine fabrics as it fell.

"Remember, we are respectable people in this respectable city," Halvard said. I dodged a boy chasing after a ball.

"In daylight, maybe."

"I *do* hope you remember what civility is, Shandar."

"Of course, it's surrounding us now," I said. "A stark contrast to the nighttime activities."

"The unmentionables," Halvard replied, holding up a

finger to shush me. "Don't speak a word about it anymore."

I raised an eyebrow and smirked.

"As your majesty wishes."

The doctor's office sat at the bottom floor of a two-story house, where the overly kind Doctor Howell lived and worked comfortably. A young servant, a boy of sixteen or so, let us in.

Behind a messy mahogany desk sat the good doctor, peering over his glasses and smiling wide.

"Mr. Vrana," he greeted, his young-ish face bursting with a radiant cheer that could have blinded the miserable. "Thank you so much for coming in."

"Wonderful to see you again, doctor," Halvard replied. "This is my brother, Shandar. You remember him, of course?"

"Ah, I do," the doctor said as he shook my hand. Firm grip, he had. Perhaps the excitement of the moment, or his youth. "How are things at your home?"

"Quiet, very quiet," Halvard said, taking a seat.

"Hm. Grief is a curious thing. It can take the smallest sliver of emotion and expand it tenfold."

I used this opportunity to snag a small biscuit that sat on the center table in a bowl. I prayed that it wasn't too old as I nibbled at it. My brother and the doctor spoke about the new maid that was being hired.

"I'd very much like you to tell me about her. And I would like to speak with her as well," Halvard said.

"The poor dear is still asleep; I hadn't expected you so early," the doctor explained. Halvard nodded, then attempted to confirm his suspicions.

"Did you say that she is from the city?"

"Found in the city, likely not born here," the doctor explained. "Someone came across her in the street late at night some weeks ago, badly injured and unable to speak, presumably due to the supposed attack that she endured. I, uh, failed to mention this last night, as I didn't want to make a stir."

I stopped chewing for a moment. By god, did that sound awfully familiar. The mangled thing, outside of the baker's shop, at nearly two in the morning. A feeling of discomfort rose in my stomach as I realized this. Suddenly the biscuit tasted stale.

"She...she was the first case?" my brother asked.

"Attacked, not murdered," Doctor Howell said. "I can assure you that she is able-bodied." There was a pause. Both my brother and I locked eyes and thought of Violet. She'd surely want to take the girl in even more so now. The doctor cleared his throat and continued. "If I'm not mistaken, and forgive my lack of research on the subject, given the way her complexion lines up, I would assume that she was born a native of our region of Skadi." Halvard didn't respond to this. I kicked at his leg, mouthing the words, "be civil". The doctor continued again, now nervous. "She doesn't speak a great deal, which may be both a blessing and a curse. I would highly recommend not being too difficult on her for the first few days, as she's not quite assimilated into the Asterbury lifestyle."

"We will be sure to help her accommodate," Halvard said, a strange disdain lacing his voice.

"Excellent, excellent. Enough of me, though, I'm sure you'd like to speak with her."

"Yes, yes, if she's decent and awake."

"Very well. I'll fetch her for you. One moment."

The doctor scurried out, calling the girl's name. *Romilla*, he called. *Romilla*. Pretty little name for a pretty little girl.

"Nervous to hire a new girl?" I asked, joking about my brother's strange behavior.

"Not in the slightest," he said. "Her mysterious background is what makes me nervous."

"Come off it, she's a harmless snow dweller," I said.

The girl came in, formally presented by the doctor as if she were his own daughter. Halvard stood up and tugged his cloak around his body a bit tighter. I stood up as well, wiping the crumbs from the corners of my mouth. She was quite the little doll, with rich brown hair and eyes. I doubted she could be over the age of seventeen. Two parallel scars lined her cheek. My mind went back to the night on the street, the night on which-and it was undoubtedly so now- she had recolored the snow around her. *Painted the town red*, I thought morbidly.

My brother, on the other hand, took a moment to look at the girl. He seemed fixated on her facial features. If I didn't know better, I would say he gave her the same look of recognition as me.

"Lovely to see you again, Romilla." Halvard said. The girl nodded in reply.

"You...you as well, Master Vrana."

"This is Master Shandar, my brother."

"I'm pleased to meet you," Romilla said.

"And I you," I replied. I fixed my gaze on her. There was, perhaps, the slightest bit of a connection when we locked eyes. Halvard cleared his throat and went on.

"You'll soon be able to meet the rest of the household when we return. My wife will be giving most of the orders."

"Yes, sir."

There was an accent somewhere in that young voice. Anyone could have missed it. The doctor was right; she hardly spoke at all. I wanted to hear her voice more.

"Are there any medical concerns?" Halvard asked both the doctor and the girl. Romilla looked at the doctor, unable to answer the question for herself.

"Nothing too worrisome nor affecting her ability to work," the doctor replied. "Only a few healing wounds that may still need treatment from time to time. I'll be more than happy to visit in order to take care of that."

"Very good. Now, Romilla, are you ready for work? We should be going."

Romilla smiled for the first time.

"I'm delighted to be of use, Master Vrana."

There was a grateful spirit that overwhelmed her quiet tone of voice. It was a youthful hope. Thankful. Creating a new life, and all that. It was an intriguing thing to hear.

"You'll do just fine, Romilla," my brother said, straight faced as ever. "That will be all, doctor."

"Do keep in good health, Masters Vrana. Romilla, I'm so glad to have been of help to you. You be good, and stay in touch, you understand?"

"Yes, doctor. Thank you."

We bid the doctor goodbye and got into the carriage as the snow began to fall faster. We went off and headed back home, with a strange and quiet girl looking down at her hands. While we rode through the city and to the outskirts, where my brother's house sat, Romilla had a curious look in her eyes for the entirety of the way there. Halvard caught me staring, and gave me a look of warning. But when I looked back at him, he stared at the girl the same way that I did. I lightly kicked him as a response.

⋈

Once we arrived, Halvard brought the girl inside and introduced her first to the staff of the kitchen, where she would be working.

"Romilla, this is Agatha, our cook," my brother introduced. "Agatha, this is Romilla, our new kitchen maid. I'm leaving her in your charge."

"Oh, I'm charmed," Agatha replied, her rosy cheeks becoming round with a jolly smile. "Heavens, you're quite a pretty li'l thing, aren't you?"

Romilla caught the energy that the woman radiated, producing a smile. Agatha, though she was a woman of troubled background, remained a happy and gentle cook. She never complained and never rose her voice unless she couldn't stop herself from laughing. Romilla, though she had never seen the woman once in her life before, picked up on this the instant she met her.

"I'm very pleased to meet you," the girl said.

"Now, that's what I like to see, a smile," the woman said in reply. "You're frightfully thin, dearie. I'll fix you up right. Try a biscuit, they're fresh."

The cook motioned to a counter where a tray of cookies sat, freshly baked. Romilla looked at Halvard, as if she were asking for approval. He nodded.

"Go on, you must be hungry," he said.

With subdued glee, Romilla went to the counter for her treat.

"What a precious little thing, bless her," Agatha said to Halvard. "We'll ge' along just fine, I'm sure."

"There's no one you don't get along with, Agatha," my brother said.

"Oh, you know I'd never pick a fight, Master Halvard," the woman chuckled. "I'm sure Romilla will enjoy her time here."

As she said this, Romilla came back, her cheeks full of perhaps more biscuits than she was allowed. Agatha laughed heartily. Both the girl and the cook even forced the slightest smile from my brother.

"Ho! Hungry little thing, you are, little chipmunk!" Agatha said, wiping tears of laughter from her eyes. "I like this one, Master Halvard."

"I thought you might."

Halvard continued on with the tour of the house, introducing the girl to the footmen, the housemaids, and Charles, the butler. My brother seemed tired out from the ordeal, but she had yet to meet the most important member of the house.

"Violet?"

"Yes?"

"The new maid is here."

"Romilla? Bring her in."

The two entered the study, where Violet sat upright at her desk, clearing her throat and standing up to greet the girl.

"Romilla, Violet issues most of the orders around the house," the man said.

"As well as I can, given recent events," the woman mumbled. "I do apologize, Romilla. Everyone in the house is still mourning dear Lizabet. Things aren't as they usually are."

Romilla only nodded. Violet furrowed her brow at the silent reply.

"You're allowed to speak, my dear," she said.

"She's very quiet, as Doctor Howell said."

Violet looked back at the girl. Romilla was staring at the ground, her hands clasped behind her back.

"It's all right, Romilla, you've nothing to be afraid of here," Violet soothed. The woman shivered. "I can assure you you'll be working with good, honest people. Chin up, now."

Romilla lifted her eyes, and not her chin. She smiled.

"Halvard, darling, take her into the kitchen to begin work," Violet said. "She'll do well under the care of Agatha."

"Yes, dear," Halvard replied.

"Very good," the woman said, sitting back down in her chair. Halvard and Romilla began to walk out of the room, when Sullivan brushed past them.

"Mother, have you seen my-"

Everyone in the room turned to see the boy, who stopped talking at the sight of Romilla.

"Oh, apologies for interrupting," he said, beginning to back away.

"No, dear, you've come at a good time. Sullivan, this is our new kitchen maid, Romilla," Violet said, gesturing to the girl.

"Oh, of course," the boy replied. Romilla, being polite, continued with her recited greeting.

"I'm pleased to meet you."

The boy stepped into the room slowly.

"As am I," Sullivan replied. When he took a closer

look at her face, my nephew frowned. There were two long scars running down her cheek. He continued with a rushed polite inquiry. "Ah, where are you from, Romilla?"

Romilla, with a childlike sense of immediate trust, looked up at Halvard for him to answer. Surprised at the girl's action, he did.

"She's a native of Skadi, Sullivan," Halvard answered. "Found in Asterbury, battered terribly."

The boy raised his eyebrows. Of course, the story sounded just as familiar to him as it did to me.

"How...how dreadful."

"Yes. She starts work with us today, so excuse us."

Sullivan watched as they headed back towards the kitchen. Perhaps it disturbed the boy slightly, seeing the girl, the bloodied, nearly-dead girl that he'd seen some time ago, on her feet and, frankly, alive.

Chapter 7

"He still refuses, mistress."

Nalia paced back and forth, biting down on her index finger. She mumbled nonsense to herself.

"Oh, but he must," she said. "How can he refuse? He can't. Not me."

Petimus shook his head and looked at his companion, who slept peacefully at his side. He sighed with relief, grateful that Nalia's anger wasn't being directed not towards him, but towards the vessel of the shadows, Halvard.

"You took his maid?"

"One of many, mistress, but he remains stubborn."

"Stubborn. What an act of foolishness. Foolish boy. What is he to gain from that? No such glory as what I can give him."

Petimus shrugged, creating a series of horrible popping from his joints.

"He doesn't wish to see you, perhaps."

"Ha!"

Nalia laughed bitterly at the very idea, the very audacious idea that the one she'd gifted with incredible power refused to express gratitude in any way. She tossed her feathered cloak over her shoulders and ran outside, letting a cold burst of air into her cabin, waking up a sleeping Verdorben. Petimus clicked his tongue at the cur and followed Nalia.

"No one refuses me. My wishes. No one can. No one will. Not when I've got him as my own."

As she said this, Nalia bent down and swept her arms along the powdery snow that her feet sank into. The snow came up in little clouds at her sides. Petimus watched her curiously, since she continuously brushed the snow away.

"My lady, do you need-"

"You stay back, fiend!" she barked at the advancing Petimus, who cowered immediately. Verdorben did the same, whimpering as the woman brushed the snow away faster and faster. Finally, she stopped, and the clouds of snow at her feet vanished. "There," she said, the frozen leaves and sticks at her feet now revealed. "Now, watch."

The witch muttered unintelligible things, bending over the ground and circling her hands and fingers all around. She muttered and gestured, muttered and gestured, muttered and gestured until she lifted both of her hands into the air above her head. A tall and human like figure appeared in front of her, rising up with the movement of her hands.

"Ahh, little one," she said with a giggle, throwing her arms around the dark figure. "Turn for Petimus to see you."

The thing turned slowly around, a black smoke-like substance exiting its ears, nostrils, and mouth. It looked very similar in gauntness and gray-skinnedness as Petimus himself, though it stood upright. Being used to the sight, the beggar shrugged.

"'Tis nothing but a shadow man," he commented, poking it with a bony finger. Verdorben sniffed at it. "A silly thing. Stupid. No brains."

Upon hearing the insults, the figure seized Petimus by the throat, lifting him into the air. Petimus choked, clawing at the thing's hands. Nalia stepped up to the creature that clutched her closest henchman.

"You are no longer the only one of your people who can kill," Nalia said, her voice a vicious whisper. "I can command them now. Took too long. Haven't done this since I brought you, my first. They can maim. They can tear apart. They can destroy at my very word. At hearing my voice."

The thing dropped Petimus, who crumpled to the ground, letting out disgusting wet coughing sounds. Nalia stepped towards him and grabbed him by the arm.

"Get him back. Bring my Halvard. My king. Or you and the cur are finished, and not by my hands. But by all of my creations. They can squeeze the life from you both, take your feeble bodies and crush them."

Petimus, just as he was about to agree, heard the faintest sound. Like a song being sung. It seemed to be a serenade, luring him away from the witch. His body dribbled into the ground as a shadow, as did Verdorben's, and the two shadows rushed away from Nalia and out of the woods.

※

One person I had not seen in the midst of my own misery in those days was my nephew. Today, I looked all over for him, to find him buried in his room, flipping through a tiny book.

"And what prompted such intellectual behavior?"

Sullivan, caught off-guard by me sneaking into his room (though I had knocked a few times), snapped his little book shut and put it to his side. I lit myself a cigarette and sat at the end of his bed.

"Not intellectual," he said, relieved to see his handsome uncle. "These are only legends."

"That's not an answer to my question," I replied.

"Curiosity, then," the boy said, getting up to close the door. I used this chance to pick up the little book. I recognized the grim purple cover.

"*An Incomplete Compendium of the Reditum*," I read. I smiled as a wave of memories came over me. "This was your father's personal handbook as a boy. Clutched at it wherever he went."

"Was it?" Sullivan said. "I wondered whose handwriting that was."

"Likely his. How did you come across it?"

"The library," my nephew replied. "One of the maids found it in a pile of books. Looks as though it hasn't been touched since it was left all the way in the back."

"I'd imagine your father would be quite pleased to see this again," I said, picking the book up and feeling the aged leather cover and letters on the front. Plain little thing, not much to it besides a crude illustration of an eye on the cover. Evidently the writer simply went by the name of "Pravda". It was the size of a pocket book, with great care taken to keep it as intact as possible. Some dust remained in the crevices between the pages as I flipped through them.

"My father's handwriting isn't too easy to read in there. Not always."

"So I've noticed," I mumbled, frowning at the scratches of ink. Notes were written alongside things such as the common wildlife in the woods, the types of trees and berries, the supposed evils lurking about that took the form of witches and shadows and cannibalistic native tribes.

"Terrifying things in here," I said as I passed an illustration of a monstrous-looking wolf.

"Why tell such tales?" my nephew asked, his childishness dripping through his voice.

"Likely to keep people from getting lost in the forest like your father did," I answered, continuing to flip through the pages. "I suppose that's why he wrote in this book; to try and find the things that were recorded in here."

I looked at the boy's all-too-innocent face. He'd never been told.

"My father's been lost in the Reditum? And he survived?"

"Oh yes, your father would frequent the outskirts, getting close to the edge of the forest," I said. "Only one day did he become so engrossed in studying the phenomenon that he became lost for days. Your poor grandmother thought she'd never see him again, until he returned, of course."

"Did anything happen to him?"

"Nothing that he's told me," I said. "He never spoke of the forest again, after it happened. He was deathly silent for months afterwards. Couldn't bear to tell anyone what had happened to him. Many were rather surprised he's kept his composure afterwards." Sullivan said nothing. "Personally, I wondered how he managed to escape alive at all," I recalled. "No one was supposed to return from the forest." The boy nodded, fascinated by his father's dark past secret.

"That's how the stories go, it seems."

I grunted in agreement as I came across a familiar page. I smiled at the block of printed text.

"I remember reading some lines from this aloud rather often," I chuckled. "I'd snatch the book from your father and tease him about it, in hopes that I'd scare him."

"Did it?"

"Oh, hardly," I replied. "He always took it back before I could read the entirety of it. Seemed more concerned about me holding the book than the words themselves."

I read it aloud, fully, to my nephew.

"Beware the beggar, little one,
Beware his sharpened gaze.
Beware his eyes like a hungry snake,
And his touch like torn, rough lace.
'Penny for the poor?
he hisses, arm outstretched,
'Or a bone for me poor little pup?'
Look away, little one,
don't give in to his plea,
don't place precious things in his cup.
Alas, it's too late
your young life is now ruined
you've caught his golden green eyes.
Don't scream as he seizes
he'll do as he pleases,
tearing through you with claws made of lies.
'Come here,' he demands, gruesomely smiling,
'Come play with me sweet little hound.'
You look at the cur
that lacks any fur,
See, it's nothing but bone all around.
Beware the beggar, little one,
Beware all his false claims.
Lo, something else lurks,

*For whom the thing works,
The Collector of miserable pain."*

I started feeling nostalgic as Sullivan appeared as fascinated as a small child upon hearing the whimsically gruesome poem. I was glad he didn't attempt to snatch away the book like his father would as a child.

"Never heard that one?"

"I've heard rumors of a beggar when I was young, but never those lines," he murmured. "I haven't seen that page yet."

I skimmed a bit more through that page, reading the text after the poem.

"Says here the beggar has been by the side of the witches and tribes for centuries," I said. "Here - *'Rumor has it, though unconfirmed, that the beggar was the very first shambled attempt at rising the dead from their graves using witchcraft. Since the time he was created, he's lurked in the woods, luring and taking any human being that happened across him and his vicious canine accomplice.'*"

My nephew looked at me. How he thought himself to be a grown man is beyond me, he looked far too much like the curious child that he was years back. Eyes wide with horror and awe. I smirked. What a darling.

"How is it that I've never heard these legends in full?" he mumbled.

"Your father likely didn't want you believing in nonsensical fairy tales," I dismissed with the wave of a hand. "As much as it pains me to compliment my little brother, he's quite sensible. Wanted to raise a strapping, logical young man."

"I suppose."

I flipped to the very back of the book, where one line was written:

Thank you, Jura.

There had been no mention of any Jura in the book, as far as I'd seen-not a plant, nor an animal, nor a monster.

What fantasy had my young brother concocted during his journey? I was curious, but at that moment, someone knocked on the door. Sullivan grabbed the book from me and stuffed it under his pillow.

"I'd like to read more," he explained quietly. "Thank you for telling me, Uncle Shandar. Don't tell my father or anyone else I have this."

"Of course," I replied, making my way to the door. I almost felt guilty for revealing my brother's past to his son, but it only seemed right to let the boy know. I couldn't wrap my head around why my brother would want to hide it in the first place.

※

Sullivan got to the edge of his bed as I left the room.

"Come in," he called. Isabelle and Romilla both came in, the latter holding a tea tray.

"Good morning, Master Sullivan," they said in harmony.

"Good morning, Isabelle. Morning, uh . . ."

"Romilla, sir," the girl replied, her voice almost a whisper.

"Romilla. My apologies."

"This is her first full day on the job, Master Sullivan," Isabelle explained. "Do as he tells you, Romilla."

"Ah, you can set the tray on this side-table. And pour the cup of tea, please," the boy said, tapping the top of the table. Upon seeing Isabelle give her an encouraging nod, Romilla carefully set the tray down and began pouring the hot tea. Unbeknownst to her, Sullivan stared at her. He squinted, trying to get a good look at her features. He remembered what his father said about her-she was a native, found in the city. She looked to be the right age, and she certainly had the scars to show for it. She must have been the one they'd found in the city. But what if those scars were from something else? His Uncle Shandar was there with him that night, perhaps he might know something about the girl. He'd gone to pick her up, after all. Lovely little thing, she was, as well. Wide brown eyes and lovely long brown hair.

"Will there be anything else, Master Sullivan?"

"Hm? Oh, uh...Isabelle, would you run along and tell my mother that my piano lesson is today? I'd like a quick word with Romilla, here."

Isabelle squinted at the boy, clearly not approving of his request. However, she never stepped out of line when it came to the master's request.

"I will be back very directly," she said. "*Very* directly." Isabelle left. Sullivan turned to the young maid.

"Romilla," he started. "That's a very nice name. Elegant."

"Th-thank you," the girl replied with a bow. "Thank you, Master."

Sullivan stood up from the bed and took a sip of his tea.

"And this tea is wonderful. Is this your doing?"

"No, sir, Miss Agatha's," Romilla said. "I, erm, can't make tea."

"Ah...Well, are you happy to be working with her?"

"Oh, yes, sir, she's wonderful."

"Very jolly woman, very happy indeed."

"Yes, sir."

There was a quick pause as Sullivan sipped again. Romilla's eyes kept flashing back to the door, at which she expected Isabelle to return and give more instructions. Sullivan, not wanting to dance around the subject too much more, asked the question that burned in his mind since the moment he'd set eyes on the girl.

"Romilla, was...was that you in Asterbury, lying on the ground? I believe my uncle and I passed by that night."

Romilla stared at her hands. She intertwined her fingers, pulled them apart, and repeated the process.

"Romilla?"

"Y-yes, master."

My nephew stared at her cheek, the one with the scars. A tear rolled past them. My nephew realized he'd made the girl uncomfortable.

"Oh, oh, please don't cry, I'm so sorry," the boy stuttered, reaching for his hanky. "Here, dry your eyes."

Before Romilla took the hanky, she used the back of her hand to wipe the tears from her cheeks. She looked at the cloth for a moment, took it, and gingerly rubbed at her eyes with it.

"I didn't mean to make you cry," Sullivan continued. "I just wanted to know if you could tell me what happened."

Freshly educated on some of the mysteries of the woods, Sullivan's childlike mind speculated whimsical things about this possible attacker. Though a more logical part of him wondered if the attacker had been a wolf, or just a crazed man running rampant throughout the area. Any possibility still proved to be terrifying.

"I...I don't know," she answered, only half truthfully. "I can't recall."

"Can you tell me if it was a man or a beast?"

"It..." Romilla's voice faded away and more tears began to spill from her soft eyes. "I'm sorry, master," she said in broken tones.

"No, no, I'm the one who should apologize," my nephew said, realizing the girl's memories were likely painful. Not to mention Isabelle would come back at any moment and see the new maid in tears. Cursing himself, he took the hanky from her hand and wiped the tears for her. "Please don't cry, Romilla."

"Yes, sir," she said through sniffles. "I'm sorry, sir, please forgive me."

"You've nothing to be sorry for," Sullivan explained, placing his hand under her chin. "Your pretty eyes should never have tears coming from them."

"Master Sullivan, if you please!" came a voice from the door.

Sullivan pulled his hand away from the girl to see a

stern-looking Isabelle in the doorway. He grinned and chuckled nervously.

"Ah, merely a friendly conversation, Isabelle," he said. "I'm just trying to get to know the new girl."

"Begging your pardon, sir, but I should hope your intentions are nothing but respectful to the new maid," Isabelle shot back. "Or your father will hear about this behavior. It won't be tolerated, just as it wasn't tolerated with your uncle some time ago. Look, the poor thing is cryin'!"

Sullivan felt the strong urge to protest that he'd done nothing inherently wrong, but he had indeed made Romilla cry.

"I do apologize, Romilla," he said. "I hope I can make it up to you." Isabelle paraded out of the room, consoling Romilla and completely ignoring the sincere apology of my nephew. Sullivan flopped back onto his bed, the guilt now overwhelming his curiosity.

❦

"What did he say to you?" Isabelle asked Romilla as they left the room. "I knew that boy was becoming too much like his nasty uncle."

"He asked ...he asked if I'm enjoying the work," Romilla replied, "If I like working under Miss Agatha."

"Then why are you crying, dearie?"

Poor Romilla wiped at her eyes, frantically trying to come up with an excuse that would not further this discussion.

"I'm...I'm just so happy to be here with him and Master Halvard and Miss Violet," she said, her accent thickening as she stumbled to find the right words.

"Well, if you say so, dear. Be warned, though, he's a cheeky one, you might have to keep a sharp eye on him. Takes after his Uncle Shandar. Both rather enjoy the occasional pretty woman that comes into their sight. Don't let your guard down, or they'll try and catch you."

Little did Isabelle realize that not a single word that she spoke in that moment made much sense to the young girl. But whatever the woman said sounded rather serious, so the girl nodded after every sentence. Though it's possible Romilla disagreed with everything the woman was saying.

I know I would have, myself.

"Well, let's get back to the kitchen," the woman said. "Agatha, Romilla is ready to begin her duties with you!"

"Oh, splendid!" the happy cook said in reply, turning from her pot to look at Romilla. "I'll take good care o' her, Isabelle."

Once Isabelle left, Agatha put Romilla to work. Small tasks, for the most part, as a scullery maid. Romilla proved her worth as a good cleaner on the first day. She scrubbed dishes, counters, swept the floor, and other such menial kitchen tasks. She only paused when she overheard a few of the other maids gossiping among themselves.

"Pay them no mind," Agatha said as she saw Romilla stop her sweeping to listen to the words of the whisperers. "We were struck with tragedy not long ago, when our dear friend Lizabet disappeared. Some say she was killed, others say she ran off. There's been no sign of her ever since. They all like to keep themselves wrapped in such tales."

"Agatha, did you not hear our new story?" one older maid, Mary, asked as she overheard Agatha speaking to Romilla. "Didja notice, when she never came back, who did?"

The cook set down the pot she'd been throwing ingredients into.

"What are you twittering on about, Mary?" she asked.

"Master Halvard, Agatha," Mary replied, her eyes large, as if she'd discovered a hidden secret. A hidden conspiracy. "Master Halvard came back from the scene, alive."

Everyone paused as Agatha narrowed her eyes and

her smile vanished. The insinuated accusation of their master lingered in the air.

"I won't be having that sort of talk of the master in my kitchen, Mary," the cook said in an attempt to dismantle it. "We have new recruits, we musn't taint her ears with silly gossip. Besides, you know the master better than I, he'd never do such a thing."

"It's highly possible, you know," Mary mumbled. "Master Halvard always did seem a bit quiet after the woods. A bit different. Isolated. How are we to know that he's not been...going mad?"

"We aren't to speak of the woods, Mary, or the master. He's done nothin' but take care of us, we must do what he asks. You know this."

Mary glanced over at the other girls, who glanced at Romilla, who cowered behind Agatha. It was a strange thing, seeing the jolly cook's muscles so tense, her face flushed with aggravation, and her fists clenched into round balls at her sides.

"Begging your pardon miss Agatha, but isn't it...a bit odd that he's been keepin' to himself so much?"

"He's done so since he was a boy, Mary, you know this just as well as I do. And this is your final warning."

Mary's voice turned into a low grumble as she started to turn around and continue working. The others joined her, and Romilla started hastily sweeping, understanding the tension as it wafted through the air like a rancid odor. Mary mumbled to the young girl next to her.

"We're all gonna be expected to keep quiet 'bout the whole thing."

Agatha slapped a large hand on the table next to her, fed up with the gossip.

"Because it is absolute poppycock and rubbish, Mary!" Agatha scolded, whirling around with a large wooden spoon in her hand. "You oughta be ashamed o' yourself, coming up with horrible stories like that, and of Master Halvard no less! Why, he'd never hurt a fly, let alone do something as horrible as what you're implying with your ridiculous tall tales!"

The kitchen went silent after Agatha yelled. Romilla stared behind the cook, as did the rest of the maids. Agatha turned to see the tall, dark master of the house himself with a small slip of paper between his fingers.

"A note from my wife," he said cautiously, handing Agatha the slip. "See to it that her orders are followed."

He walked past the flustered cook and calmly addressed the rest of the kitchen. All of the women, both young and old, looked down at their feet, some fidgeting, others with their hands clasped anxiously behind their backs.

"I'm not sure what exactly you ladies are saying in regards to me, but if it doesn't come to an end there will be repercussions of great scale." Every one of the maids nodded in response. "Now back to work, all of you. Do not let this happen again."

When the kitchen began bustling with activity again, Halvard turned to Romilla, who seemed rather on edge.

"My apologies, Romilla, I understand you are new. But let it be known that this sort of behavior is not acceptable in my home."

"Yes, sir."

"Nothing against me in my own home shall be tolerated, is that very clear?"

"Y-yes, Master Halvard."

He paused for a moment. The slightest flash of something familiar caught his eye as she looked up at him. Halvard could see something in the girl's eyes, a thread of fear tugging at her being. A permanent timidity. A nervousness inflicted by something over time. Perhaps her whole life. That nervousness, the same dread that followed Halvard everywhere he went - somehow he could see it in her eyes.

"Romilla, have we met before the funeral?"

The girl shook her head.

"The funeral was the first I saw of you, Master

Halvard."

The master of the house only pursed his lips. He knew her from somewhere. Surely she was a native of the Reditum. A native of the darkness.

A native, perhaps, to something more sinister than the innocent and childlike game that she played.

"Of course, of course. Carry on, my dear."

Chapter 8

Halvard did not feel his best during that night. At first, he thought too much of the new maid, Romilla, and her uncanny resemblance to someone else he'd seen before. It made sense, after all, considering her native roots. As the night went on, however, he tossed and turned in his bed, a horrible feeling creeping into his mind, like the instinct of dread that many contract when something is about to go horribly wrong. That dread consumed the poor man, washing over his being from his head to his gut. He told his dear wife that he felt the slightest bit ill, like something he'd eaten had started sitting like a rock in his bowels.

In truth, my friend, my brother was not ill. He felt that something had infiltrated the sanctuary of his home. He got up to take a midnight walk, something he'd been known to do since he was a young boy, but only around the house. When he felt dizzy from the nauseating worry, Halvard went into the empty study and took a slow and cautious seat in the armchair. The fireplace was not lit, and neither were the lamps. There was an enveloping darkness that oozed into every corner of the room. When a wave of nausea hit him again, he-curiously enough-cupped his hands and scooped the air as though he were taking water from a pond to drink. He "poured" the nothing into the air a little off to the side, then repeated the process. Over and over he picked up the black shadows and poured them over nothing, growing more impatient and more furious as he continued to repeat the motion.

"Where are you?" he hissed.

He took one last bit of shadow and, instead of "pouring" it, let the blackness run through his fingers. A patch of light opened up on the floor, where a single reptilian eye peered up at the dark man through the break in the shadows.

"Fancy seeing you here, darling," a raspy voice said.

"Bloody hell," Halvard gasped, jumping out of the

chair at the sudden jarring sight. The figure of Petimus rose up through the floor with a growling Verdorben, having been found. His back cracked into a hunch, and his smile nearly parted his whole face. The corpse, despite the fact that he lacked any muscles, struck a found match over his nearly exposed shoulder bone. Verdorben let out a snarl and sat on his haunches.

"Careful with the shadows, Halvard, they stain."

Halvard looked at his hands, which did indeed appear as though he had spilled ink all over them. He hastily wiped them on his dark purple bathrobe, hoping the black would come off.

"Why have you come back?" my brother asked, checking his palms for inky shadows.

"Someone brought me here," Petimus cackled, running his fingers through the non-existent fur on the cur's head. "Not certain who, but someone recited my poem. I wondered if it was you, telling me you've finally agreed to Nalia's deal." The poorly lit corpse dropped the dying match into an oil lamp that sat on the side-table next to the armchair. The lamp burst to life, giving a better light, though not much.

Halvard's stomach dropped even further than it was before.

"Who could have-?"

"'Twas nothing but a reminder of my job, anyway," Petimus said. "To fetch you for Nalia and stop at nothing to do so."

"Why?"

"She gave you a gift, Master Halvard," Petimus replied, taking Halvard's hand in his own clawed, bony fingers. Halvard jerked his hand away at the sudden cold, dead feeling. "A gift that she only bestowed upon you under the condition that you use it for her."

Halvard looked at the black streaks on his hands as they danced in the flickering lamplight. "She has given me no gifts in all the time I knew the witch."

"This power of yours is not a gift?"

Halvard sat back down in the chair and touched the flickering shadow on the table with one finger, holding it still, then released his finger, letting it dance around once again. The shadow seeped up into his fingertip like a gravity-defying liquid.

"It's a curse. It's...it's not natural."

"Call it what you like, boy," Petimus said, scratching a spot where an ear should have been. "Whatever it may be, Nalia only gave it to you so that you could return the favor someday."

"The only way for me to return this 'favor' is to kill the woman."

"You'll not touch the shadow people," Petimus said, his tone growing more serious and less mischievous. "She needs your aid, Halvard."

"I'm not helping that witch."

"You don't seem to understand how hospitable she was to you, boy."

Halvard stopped playing with the shadow. A mix of emotion hit him, a stomach-churning combination of anger, fear, and memories that suddenly resurfaced. He could hear his own screaming from that night echoing through the woods.

"Her disgusting display was not hospitality!" he hissed, his level-headedness quickly turning into an irrational, trauma-induced rage. A dribbling trickle of black began to creep from his ear to his neck.

"More hospitable than killing you," Petimus retorted, "as she does with every Reditum wanderer."

"Why me?" Halvard asked angrily, ignoring the black rivulets dripping down both sides of his neck. "Why couldn't she have just killed me like all the rest?!"

"She felt you were special, boy."

"I'm no different than the rest of them!"

"You are now."

With a cry of anguish, Halvard knocked the table

forward in an attempt to injure the corpse. Petimus and Verdorben dodged and let the table and its contents fall with a loud crash. Halvard realized what he'd done and looked into the hall, hoping no one had heard the sound.

"Very well," Petimus said, a sickening grin crossing the thing's face, splitting it nearly in two. "If you won't come with me now to appease the great Nalia, I suppose I'll be forced to stay here for a while."

"You're not staying here."

"We shall stay here and slowly take what's yours," Petimus said. "One by one. Little by little. Until you finally agree to come with me."

As he said these final words, both he and Verdorben disappeared into the shadows. Halvard took the lamp and searched the room, but there was no sign of them.

Who could have read that poem?

Chapter 9

I'd wandered into the dining-room one afternoon, hungry. After requesting a small lunch and taking a seat, I heard some of the maids whispering among themselves. Curious, I tried to eavesdrop to the best of my ability, until Romilla brought out a bowl of soup for me.

"Quiet in there, hm?" I asked her.

"Oh...yes, sir," Romilla replied with her soft and sweet voice.

"And what would all of you lovely ladies be so intrigued about, pray tell?"

Romilla's eyes got rather wide when I requested to know what the gossip was about. She shook her head.

"Forgive me, Master Shandar, but I-I don't think that I can tell you."

I leaned in closer to her, placing a hand on my thin knee. I noticed that I, seated, was as tall as her. She backed up slightly, alarmed by the motion.

"Now, I'm a master of this house as well, Romilla," I lied. "It's important that you bring anything such as this to my attention. But, I promise you I will not tell a soul."

Of course, I only wished to know what the gossip seemed to be about. After all, who wouldn't have been curious of the drama within their own home?

"Well . . ." Romilla's wide eyes darted around the room, not wanting to get caught revealing secrets to the most handsome person in the house. "Some of the women think that Master Halvard may have had something to do with Lizabet's death," she said. My eyebrows went up. As many rumors as I'd heard in past years, this certainly caught me by surprise. I sank back into my chair and rested my chin in my hand.

"Well, isn't that interesting?"

"I don't believe it," Romilla said quickly, as though trying to redeem herself. "Master Halvard has been too kind to me."

I nodded.

"You're right to avoid such gossip," I said, stirring up the soup with a spoon. "You're a well-behaved little thing, Romilla. It's a shame there's not more girls like you in this world."

I sipped my soup after I felt goosebumps prickling my sleeves. I felt chilly.

"I...perhaps not," Romilla stammered, rubbing her arm. "Is there anything else I can do for you, sir?"

I looked up at the fireplace which, to my correct assumption, had begun to dim.

"Tend to the fire, if you please, this room's quite drafty. Cold."

Romilla nodded and scurried over to the fireplace, pulling a poker from its spot. She began to jab at the coals and stacked wood. I continued to eat my soup when my brother walked into the room. He stopped as he saw Romilla picking at the coals carefully.

"Shandar, what is she doing?" he asked. I chuckled.

"Well, I haven't the heart to tell her she's not doing it right, poor dear is-"

"Is the fire low?"

I gave a quizzical look to my brother, whose wits at that moment seemed dimmer than the fire.

"Why not ask the girl herself?" I replied, gesturing to her. "I'm busy at the moment."

Halvard said nothing. His eyes scanned the fireplace, from Romilla, to the hearth, to the coals, to the mantle. He was intently focused on the fireplace, and I couldn't tell why. "Well, if you'd like to scold the girl, then by all means do so," I said.

The sound of a large log falling into the coals startled the both of us. Halvard lunged for Romilla and pulled her away, while I stood up. I thought that the carpet may have caught fire. But it hadn't. Halvard pushed Romilla behind him as he watched the fireplace. He yanked the poker from her hands and adjusted the kindling as needed.

"Be more careful next time," he snapped at the girl, who, bewildered and frightened, nodded.

"Y-yes, sir. I'm sorry, sir."

"Now, run off back to Agatha. You've more work to do."

Romilla did just that. I stared at my brother.

"Afraid your house will burn down?" I asked, jokingly."The stone castle?" Halvard pursed his lips and shook his head.

"Trying to keep the clumsy little thing safe," he muttered before leaning the poker against the wall and storming off. I sipped up more of my soup as he went into the foyer and disappeared.

༺༻

Later that evening, my nephew and I decided to have a walk in the cold. Perhaps it wasn't the best of decisions, but we managed to have some privacy in that way. Sullivan discussed with me the things he'd been learning in that little book of his. He pulled it from his pocket and pointed to what he was talking about.

"Umbraberries are deadly," he said, showing me the illustration. "You can tell what they look like based on their purplish color. And according to this book, the population of wolves in this forest has been exceeding dangerous numbers. See, the beginning of the book says things like this, where the handwriting starts off as neat and orderly."

"I see," I replied, paying little attention.

Handwriting, I thought. *My brother's. Why did he startle so badly at the fire today?*

"And once you get further into the book-that's where the myths and legends begin-the scribbles become more frantic and rushed."

"Goodness," I mumbled, my thoughts elsewhere. I decided to bring them to life. "Is there any mention of fire in that little book?"

"Fire, uncle?"

"I'm curious."

Sullivan flipped through the book, searching for anything of significance that had anything to do with fire.

"There's mention in the legends," he said, still searching. "I know it said something about fire-ah!"

I stopped walking and read the printed text.

"There's a fascination here with fire," I read. *"The forest becomes more alive when fires are present. Even with small fires built up for warmth, some say there's an evil lurking beneath them."*

Sullivan laughed.

"Yes, that's it. Surely you don't believe all that, do you uncle? Fire monsters?"

"Certainly not," I replied, skimming over the rest of the page. The scribbles were frantic and contained plenty of exclamations. Something about stinging eyes and seeing faces in the smoke, I think. Oh, the imagination of a child.

"I haven't been able to figure it out," Sullivan said. "I wonder if my father believed them, given this writing."

"He seemed to earlier," I said. "Jumping sky-high as the kindling shifted."

"Did he?"

"With speeds I didn't think possible for a man his age," I replied. "He pulled poor little Romilla away from the fire like it was going to attack her."

"Strange," the boy said.

"Well, do you believe such things?" I asked the boy. "After all, you've been learning quite a bit about this forest."

"I'm only entertaining the fantastic ideas, uncle Shandar," he replied, snapping the book shut. "It's the only time I've been able to learn about these legends. It's a pleasurable escape from my lessons in business."

We continued walking in silence, save for the sound of whistling winds and snow crunching under our feet. Sullivan cleared his throat.

"Perhaps that's why my father kept himself busy

with this book as well," he speculated.

"Oh, I would say so," I replied. "After all, the woods are mysterious. Who doesn't enjoy a lovely mystery to toy around with?"

We stopped at the edge of the garden, the part that overlooked the Reditum. We both stared silently at the foreboding woods, the supposed home to all of the legends contained in the small purple handbook. Whispering, chilly winds brushed the branches of the tall conifers. Sullivan let out a sigh.

"There would only be one way to find out how true these things are, uncle Shandar," he said. "Though I'm not brave enough to do so." I let out a laugh.

"I don't suppose you truly are starting to believe them, then?" I asked. The boy chuckled uneasily.

"No...no, I suppose not," he answered. I turned on my heels and walked back towards the house, while Sullivan followed behind, rather slowly.

૭૭

My nephew went back into the house and tucked the little booklet away into his vest's inside pocket. He'd decided to further study the little volume in the library. Where else might one read? Sullivan stepped inside and headed towards his favorite armchair in front of the fire. Before he could sit down, he saw his father in the seat parallel to the other, gazing almost longingly into the fire.

Perhaps "longingly" isn't the proper word. Sullivan scrutinized his father's face. Crinkled brow, as usual, but a blazing look in his eyes. Intense. Focused. The man's fingers tapped impatiently on one another. His hair looked greyer. His face? More gaunt. Sullivan, realizing he couldn't open the little book in front of his father (or, at least, he felt it best not to), still sat down slowly in the armchair. Halvard's fingers stopped tapping against each other and he looked up at his son.

"Hello, father," he greeted, his voice nearly a whisper. Halvard nodded.

"Sullivan."

The two were silent for a moment. The boy imagined many things in that moment-his father wrote the things in this book. What kind of knowledge did he possess about the Reditum woods? What things did he see? All of these questions nearly burst from Sullivan's mind, until he realized that his father tensed up even more at his presence. Halvard leaned forward, his elbows resting on his knees, breathing heavier, eyes wide open, and upper teeth gnawing at his lower lip. Surely this was the paranoid behavior that his dashing uncle Shandar referred to earlier. Halvard had never been afraid of fire before.

"I, uh...I wonder if you're all right?" the boy said, his words spilling nervously from his lips. Halvard didn't look at his son.

"Of course," he replied. "I wonder the same for you."

"Oh, I am."

Another silence ensued. Sullivan felt it necessary to continue having a conversation. He wanted answers to all of his childish questions. His mind raced frantically to phrase them without conveying too much knowledge of the things in the compendium.

"Enjoying the fire?" he asked. Halvard sighed.
"Yes."

Sullivan concluded from the lack of any sort of relaxed demeanor that his father was certainly not enjoying the fire.

"You don't seem to be."

Halvard creased his brow even more. He chewed the inside of his lip and sat up straighter.

"Do you not believe me?" he asked, still staring intently into the flashing flames.

"I...you just don't seem comfortable, is all."
"I am."

At this point, it became evident that Halvard wasn't focusing on his son at all, rather on the fire. Sullivan, slightly hurt by this realization, attempted to pull his father's attention away from the hearth.

"What do you think of Romilla?" he said, changing the subject. "She seems like quite a nice girl. Does well, Agatha says. A strong worker."

Halvard's stare narrowed, as though he spotted something intriguing in the smoke and ash.

"She's fine," he said. "Not adjusted, but fine."

The blond boy scoffed.

"Is that all? 'She's fine'?"

"Hm? Yes."

The attempt to turn this into a solid conversation left Sullivan frustrated. He thought it may be time to introduce the difficult topics - the ones that he knew would bring his father to answer. Perhaps it would enlighten the boy on some of the mysteries he wanted to unravel from the compendium.

"Do you like the view of the forest?"

Halvard took a moment before answering.

"It's nothing but trees. Dull."

"Then why live near it?" the boy asked.

"Away from people, the city," his father said. "Your mother and I wanted somewhere that wasn't full of people. I thought you knew this."

"I did," Sullivan said, "I only wondered if you liked it."

For the first time in that brief period, Halvard looked at his son.

"Liked what?"

"The Reditum."

The man focused his gaze back at the fire, sinking back into his chair.

"It's nothing but trees. Trees and wolves and...berries."

This wasn't the man displayed so clearly in the book. The handwriting, the scribbled notes, the handsome first-hand witness to testify - his father clearly lied. There must have been something there that believed even the slightest legends. Something. Even if it was the strange fire creatures. Clever boy, that Sullivan. Masterful albeit slow thinking. He chose to push further.

"Only trees? What about deer? Birds? Fantastical creatures, even?"

Of course, Halvard, being as clever as his son, glared back at him.

"What's gotten into you?" he shot back. "It's a silly forest. Animals. Plants. Snow. Nothing more or less."

"Nothing at all?" the boy said, his heart sinking ever so slightly.

"Nothing."

"What about Romilla? Isn't she a native? Don't you suppose there's others of her kind living there?"

Halvard's body became rigid.

"Don't ask me such things, I wouldn't know. Perhaps. Decide for yourself."

Frustrated at not receiving any proper answers, Sullivan sank back into his chair and watched the fire roaring away, licking at the kindling below it. It had become dimmer as he argued with his father. *Perhaps,* Sullivan thought, *if I try to recreate the scene that Uncle Shandar told me about, then I might see why he's acting this way.*

The boy stood up and cautiously reached for the fire poker.

"I'll fix this for you," he said. Just as he expected, Halvard jumped up and yanked the poker out of his son's hands.

"It doesn't need any fixing," he snapped, putting the poker back. "Let it die down. And stay away, it's dangerous to go near it."

"I'm quite old enough to adjust kindling, don't you think?"

The boy and his father stared at each other. Halvard's facial expression changed from his normal sternness to an intensely stressed expression.

"I'm just protecting my son," he answered. "And you will do as I say."

Sullivan's own childlike face soured into a look of disgust.

"Protecting me," he mocked. "As though I'm still a dainty child."

"Don't you dare start this with me, Sullivan," Halvard said, his voice a warning tone.

"Why shouldn't I? Am I not allowed to be more than a child in your eyes?"

"Sullivan-"

"You can't stand me being anything like uncle Shandar, so you'll start shunning me like you do with him?"

"Sullivan!"

"You'll start to hate me because I'm a young man doing things that you don't like, won't you? Won't you?"

Halvard affixed his gaze to the floor. He let out short breaths, as though holding in tears.

"I'll protect you from anything I want to. And you'll not challenge me, or else your punishment will be severe." He gripped Sullivan's shoulder. "Is that very clear?"

The boy's breaths grew heavier. He unclenched his teeth and fists. Halvard stared at his son, the absolute height of sternness becoming evident in every crease of his face. Sullivan stepped back and shook his father's hand from his shoulder. He knew how angry his father could get.

"Yes, sir," he mumbled before storming away. Halvard stayed behind, watching as the flames died down. He placed his face in his hands and flopped back into the chair, refusing to let the sobs out from inside his chest.

Oh, the joys of keeping secrets.

Chapter 10

"Take the pen."

Petimus held out the rough wooden ink pen in his dried-out fingers. The girl that sat in the chair, shaking and whimpering, took it from her captor's bony hand without looking.

"Now, tell me your name."

The girl didn't answer, but pursed her lips, afraid to let them part. Petimus crawled to the side-table next to her chair and started playing with her blond hair. She winced, unable to hold back the quivering sobs.

"Answer me, girl, what is your name?" Petimus repeated, his long tongue brushing against her exposed ear and neck. Verdorben held a defensive stance in front of her, panting as he stood guard.

"N-nancy, my name is Nancy!" she burst, the sobs finally escaping her tight throat.

"Nancy. How lovely," Petimus replied with a horrible giggle. Without turning his gruesome head to look, Petimus reached for the side of the table and slid the drawer open. He fished out a loose and old piece of paper, presumably some kind of business letter that remained untouched for years. He slapped it onto the table next to where he sat. "Write this down," he instructed, violently turning Nancy's head with his hand so that she faced the paper. "*I, Nancy...*"

The girl scribbled the words shakily on the paper.

"*...regrettably must resign my position as maid in the Vrana household.*"

She stopped.

"Please, I don't understand—"

"No need!" Petimus hissed, yanking her hair. "Keep writing."

She put the pen back to the paper, tears of sheer terror dripping down her face.

"*I cannot live...with the disappearance of...my good*

friend, Lizabet. Farewell."

The thing let go of Nancy and seized the paper, reading over what he'd dictated. He nodded in approval.

"Good, good," he said. "Leave it here. We'll wait for your master to retrieve it."

The maid cautiously placed the note on the table.

"But I...I'm not leaving," she said, her voice barely a whisper. Unfortunate, though, that she feared that escaping the two disgusting beings wouldn't be possible.

Petimus and Verdorben looked at each other and licked their lips. The girl shifted uncomfortably in her seat.

"We'll wait to find out," was the curt response. "In the meantime," Petimus hissed, advancing closer to the girl, who tried her best to back away, "I think we'd like to be served a meal."

The girl screamed as Petimus hopped from the table and on to her lap. He faced her, and covered up her mouth, leaning closer to her.

"Yes, yes, I disgust," he hissed. "No need to remind me."

He lurched into a sitting position on Nancy's skirt. Nancy tried to look away, to get the image of the bulging eyes and gray rib cage out of her mind. The clammy flesh on her cheek prevented it, however. As she started to struggle, Petimus put a hand around her neck and started squeezing the sides as a warning.

"Sit still for me, won't you?" he said, his palm digging into her throat as he clutched her neck. "Still, now. Stiller."

Nancy let out muffled choking sounds through the bony fingers of Petimus. Verdorben sniffed at the air, advancing towards the girl. It was as though he could smell death approaching.

Petimus watched as Nancy's eyes opened and closed, frantically searching the room, screaming for help, forming tears. He licked at his lips, trembling with anticipation.

"Be still," he whispered, putting his other hand

around her neck to accompany the first. Nancy let out a horrible gagging sound before her eyes finally rolled back and her body fell limp. Petimus opened and closed his drooling jaw.

"Retired from this household and this world," he said, stroking the former maid's hair. "Come, Verdorben. They'll see this note soon enough. And then we'll take a stroll through the city, hm?"

With somewhat ease, Petimus took the body in his arms and dragged it into the shadows of the floor, where any trace of it vanished entirely.

What a shudder it was that ran through Halvard's aging body. The same shudder, the same anxiety that constantly nagged at his brain. The one that made his mind produce that oozing black shadow in abundance. Halvard could hear it gurgling through his ear canal. He reached for the napkin on the side-table. As he did so, the man noticed his lovely wife standing in the doorway.

"Violet," he greeted, clumsily pressing the napkin to the side of his head.

"Halvard, dear," the black-haired enchantress of a woman replied, "I wondered if you'd like to come to bed. You seem out of sorts."

She took notice of the napkin pressed against his ear as she said this.

"Are you...are you all right?"

"Merely a small pain," Halvard said, getting up from his seat and glancing one last time at the fireplace. The fire was almost completely dead.

"Well, perhaps a rest will help that," Violet said, stepping closer and reaching her hands out to touch his face. "Or are you getting another fever, like last winter?"

"No fever, no," he replied, leaning back. "I'm all right, dear, no need to worry."

"There's always a reason to worry with you, your son, and your brother in the household," she said, pulling away the napkin. Halvard held back the protests and itched at his ear. Fortunately for him, the room, seeing as the nighttime was closing in and the fireplace only held faintly orange coals, was dark.

"Halvard, is this blood?"

"Yes...I hit my head," he answered quickly, taking the napkin and seeing how much "blood" had spilled into it. "Nothing to act up about."

"Oh poor thing," Violet said. "Let's get it patched then."

"No!"

A shocked silence filled the air. Violet stared at her husband, like he'd just struck her.

"I beg your pardon?" she asked. "Halvard-"

Halvard stared at the fireplace. The hot coals smoldered under the weight of the newly destroyed kindling, crackling and popping and sizzling at their will. Violet took her husband's arm.

"Darling, you need rest," she concluded, more urgent than before. "Directly."

She pulled Halvard gently out of the library, where, among those smoldering coals, a wide and disgusting grin appeared, then faded. Halvard watched helplessly as it vanished into the dark.

Chapter 11

Rumor got around the house that the elegant master Halvard had come down with something. Violet made it a point to treat it as nothing too serious, so as not to create any sort of chaos within the home. In my eyes, it may have explained his terribly disturbed behavior about fires yesterday. I deemed it logical. Whether the rest of the household did? Well, I'll point out that the maids enjoyed their share of gossiping on that day. The sickly's darling wife called for a doctor and sent maids with tea and various other remedies to her husband as she continued handling her books and accounts. I stopped into my brother's room to give him a friendly visit.

"Hi-ho, dear sick brother," I said, as happily as I could. "Another winter fever, is it?"

"There's no fever," he said through gritted teeth in the most defeated of voices. Surely, his wife had gone overboard with the care. But I'd argue it was for good reason, the man was certainly not well.

"You're suffering a headache, then?"

"Not until you entered the room," he growled.

"Ahh, come now, you know I mean well by visiting you."

"You either mean well or come to mock me," he said, sipping a minty tea.

"My wife means well. I can't say the honest same for you."

My pride wouldn't let me be hurt by this comment, but stripped down to my loving self, I might have been truly hurt by this. Maybe.

"Then I'll leave," I said. "But only if you answer me something."

"What?" I pointed at the candles lit next to him.

"Tell me, do those terrify you today?"

Halvard gave me a baffled look until he realized what I meant. His facial expression melded into a quietly furious one.

"I don't know what you mean."

Someone knocked on the door. I answered, and there stood a bright and cheery-eyed Romilla, with a bottle of medicine.

"Good morning, Master Halvard," she quipped.

"Master Shandar."

"Morning, dear," I replied. Halvard only grunted, like the cranky old man he was on his way to becoming.

"Your wife sent me with this to see if it would ease the pain before Doctor Howell arrived." Romilla placed the bottle on the side-table. She attempted a clumsy yet practiced curtsy with her apron in one hand and her dress in the other. "If you need anything, Violet says to ask me."

"No, I'm fine, dear," Halvard said. "Thank you."

Romilla placed her hands in her apron-pocket as she went near the door, and dug out a sheet of paper.

"Oh, ah..." she faced us again. "I found this. I meant to give it to Miss Violet, but-"

Halvard wasted no time in becoming cross with the poor girl.

"Sneaking business letters into your pockets is NOT a behavior that we condone, Romilla, hand that over to me right now."

"Oh, Halvard-" I started and never finished. My brother shushed me and took the paper from the girl. I rolled my eyes and addressed the now-nervous maid instead.

"Romilla, where did you find this?" I asked her gently.

"On...on the floor of the study," she said. "This morning, before Miss Violet woke. I kept it for safekeeping before I brought it to her. I'm sorry."

Halvard became distracted after reading the note multiple times. He finally looked up, looking both angry and alarmed.

94

"Shandar, bring this back to my wife. Tell her that she should communicate with me when servants are resigning their position!"

Off-put by my brother's fit, I grabbed the note and read over it myself.

"I, Nancy, regrettably must resign my position as maid in the Vrana household. I cannot live with the disappearance of my good friend, Lizabet. Farewell."

"This is completely and utterly unprofessional," Halvard fumed, getting himself up from his bed. "I'll tell her myself. What will people think, if our maids simply up and leave without a thread of notice?"

Halvard snatched the note back into his own hands and stormed out of the room. I followed him, with the frightened Romilla close behind me.

⁂

"You think this is an acceptable form of resignation?" Halvard hissed at his wife. Romilla and I only watched from the doorway, myself with a cigarette between my fingers to appear calm. Though the sweat building on my pale forehead said otherwise. Violet stood up, revealing her dark day dress and slender figure.

"I've not a clue what you're talking about!" she shouted back. "You're only waving around a scrap of paper!"

"Nancy, I'm talking about Nancy!" he shouted back, shoving the paper into her hand. "She's resigned! You can see for yourself."

After reviewing the paper a few times, Violet sank back into her study chair and let out a long sigh.

"Poor dear likely felt miserable," was the only thing she could muster.

"So she told none of us that this was happening?" Halvard said. "Nobody at all?" He looked at the doorway, where Romilla rapidly shook her head and I shook mine slowly.

"Haven't seen her since yesterday," I answered calmly.

"She wasn't sad or miserable at all," one of the servant boys chimed in, very quietly. We all looked at him. "Nancy was laughing and happy yesterday."

"Perhaps she'd just been hiding it?" Violet said. "Maybe she was-oh, I don't know what to make of this!"

Charles stepped into the doorway after lightly knocking to introduce his presence.

"Oh, come in," Violet sighed, sinking back into her chair, her head in her hand. Charles announced Doctor Howell. "Doctor," Violet greeted him, standing up immediately again. "Forgive how this looks, we've only just discovered a...strange situation."

"No need to apologize, Violet," the little man answered, taking a glance at Halvard. "Begging your pardon, Mr. Vrana, but are you not ill?"

"I am *not* ill," my brother snapped. "My wife only put me in bed because she believed so."

"Let's discuss the matter at hand, *in private*," Violet said, glaring at her husband. "Charles, please take Doctor Howell to the drawing room. Everyone else, if you could kindly leave the room."

༺༻

I sat in the drawing room with the doctor, making idle and awkward conversation with him. At a point in our dull conversation, the young and sprightly gentleman decided to stop beating about the bush.

"If you don't mind me asking, what has happened between Halvard and Violet?"

"Well, another maid of ours is...well, she's decided that she no longer wants to work for us. Resigned, gone."

"Peculiar," the doctor answered. "That is a cause for distress."

I pursed my lips as I attempted to think of something to say. Instead, I took another drag on my cigarette and stared at the wall pictures of past and present family.

"Peculiar, indeed," I said.

"And what do you think of the whole scenario?"

"Me?" I savored the taste of tobacco and set the cigarette into the ashtray. "It's...quite possible, I suppose. Logical. Supposedly she left due to the disappearance and untimely death of her poor friend, Lizabet."

"Fitting for those suffering grief," the doctor said. "Supposedly, you say?"

I lit another cigarette and puffed on it. Mother hated this nervous habit of mine.

"Supposedly," I repeated. "It's what was written on her note, the only evidence left after she took off."

The doctor shook his head.

"Curious enough, a few children went missing from the city this morning, as well. Their mothers spoke frantically with the police, but the boys never turned back up."

"Oh?"

"It was the talk of the city all morning. They'd gone to bed, and their families woke to find...nothing. Their beds were empty, save for bits of blood on one. Like...the boy had been putting up a fight."

I repeated the lines in my head. A tension filled the room. Both the doctor and I realized that this seemed far too similar to the heavy and terrifying events of last time. Eerily similar.

"Coffee, Doctor?" asked Romilla from the doorway.

⸎

Sullivan, having just finished with his business lesson of the day, sat in his soft bed and reached under his pillow for the Compendium. As he opened the aging pages at random, a small slip of paper slid out from the book and into his lap.

"Oh!" Immediately interested, Sullivan snatched the paper and unfolded it, revealing handwriting that matched the notes in the book. The boy squinted, struggling to read the fading words, but managed to make it all out:

"It's been weeks, yet I fear there's no one to hear, no one to listen to what's happened. Not a soul, not mother, father, Shandar, nor any teachers would believe what I have to relay! I must put it down! I went into the Reditum to escape my dull reality! These stories and legends were too whimsical to ignore. I had to find out for myself whether they held any truth. Monsters and shadows and witches and the like – I couldn't stand hearing of it and not seeing it with my own eyes! It took days of cold, of no food, of wandering alone! I thought for sure I'd die in that wretched place, if not for her! A native girl, a forest dweller, Jura, found me and made a fire to sit by, and brought crude raven meat to save me from starving. She seemed nervous. Quite nervous. But I thanked her, I embraced her. Until she complained of pain – then began to shout, she told me to leave, to run away, to find home again! I became afraid, too, and then I saw HER – Jura's wretched mother, Nalia! Just the picture in my mind brings me pain! The old woman screeched with disgusting glee, she'd found 'the one'! I'd no idea what she meant, until she swept me away to her hut in the woods! She spoke like a madwoman, crying out in insane joy about a 'king' and her 'people' – she frightened me so much, I tremble while writing this! After what seemed to be kindness and hospitality from her, Nalia took me into the clearing behind her hut, and sat me on a table. 'Lie down, lie down!' she screeched at me. It scared me so, Jura begged her mother to stop, but I found myself unable to resist! And then, the things I saw next – the shadows covered the sun so it looked like night! A figure with horrible reptilian eyes, one that Nalia called 'Petimus' – the beggar! Nalia recited things I couldn't hear, while Jura shouted and screamed behind her to stop! And then, the pain

– the pain that I felt! My ears, my chest! They tore open! It hurt to no end, I felt myself scream but could hardly hear it! For so long, that pain went on! It hurt! It hurt! I screamed, Jura cried, Nalia laughed like an asylum patient! Next I knew, I felt myself being pulled off that altar, and Nalia screeched as I was carried off! Jura held my hand and we ran – we ran far away, until Jura collapsed! I begged her to come with me, whilst clutching my chest, but she shouted at me to run! And I did, I ran – the pain was too much but I felt no urge to rest while I heard that horrible screeching behind me! And I ran for the whole of the day, until I heard no more screaming. It wasn't until the next day when I came back from the woods, back into the city. I've told none of this to anyone. I can't speak. My ears and chest still throb in unbearable pain, but there's no trace of injury. Every time I become angry, my ears bleed. I can still hear her voice shrieking at me, at Jura, at that creature she called her pet. I can't write any more. I can't. I will break."

    Sullivan read over the paper again. And again. And again. This was the work of a young victim of trauma. One that he'd never seen. His father would never have written something like this, surely?
    My nephew wouldn't be sleeping that night.

Chapter 12

Nancy's disappearance, though meant to be kept quiet, became the talking point of this house. Though I shouldn't say only the household, but to the police in the city. More detectives had come by to question my brother and his wife. Violet did most of the talking, however, as Halvard stood by with a look of anguish on his face. The essence of misery.

"The missing girl's family is living in the city, we've already informed them of her disappearance, and they've sent us to search the grounds and ask some questions," a stout constable said. "They're rather upset that this occurred."

"Naturally, we are as well," Violet answered with concern, but holding an upright stature. "Whatever it takes to find her. We never thought she'd run off like that."

"Seems too late to think such things now, miss, there's two missing servants of yours, six missing boys from the city, and another missing barmaid, also from the city. Not to mention one of your servants-the native girl-was the first to be targeted in this series of attacks."

"There's no connection between my house and the disappearances," Halvard interjected, his tone sharp and curt. "This attacker is targeting people in the city now, as well, you might take your business there to find this...perpetrator."

"Begging your pardon, sir, we're only following orders," the constable answered, flustered. "Nancy's father asked us to visit you directly."

"Halvard, just answer the questions," Violet mumbled. "Do as they say. Nancy's family has a right to be worried for their daughter. You'd be worried if Sullivan vanished, wouldn't you?"

"The monster is clearly coming from Asterbury," Halvard pressed, his voice rising. "Why not start your search there, and not here? Do they not realize that their city is in danger, too?"

"Halvard!" Violet whispered.

"I'll not allow such tones, Master Halvard," the constable said sternly. "I'd recommend doing as you're told, before you have far more serious matters to deal with, such as facing a judge."

"Then I'll ask you to speak with my wife, and you may let me be," Halvard growled. "Darling, give these prying fools what they want. I'll begin with tonight's supper."

"Halvard!"

My brother stormed away from the police and from his wife. He got further and further, making out the sound of Violet clumsily explaining that her husband is under a lot of stress, and lost his workers, and wasn't well - every excuse she could. Halvard felt the slightest bit of guilt as he marched off, away from his problems. He went into his own mind as he walked up the stairs. Clearly someone with malicious intent brought all this upon his house, and not just Petimus. There must have been someone else.

Not a soul in this household should know those verses, he thought. That poem was tucked away, in secret. In that book. Not a soul should have known it. Petimus and his disgusting feral accomplice were loose in the city, as well as in the Vrana home. Appearing throughout the night, carrying off whomever they pleased. Was it someone in the city who'd brought him? No, no, surely not. Someone in this house, Petimus had said. Someone here. They'd summoned him, read the entire thing out loud. Forced him here. To teach Halvard a lesson? To bring him into the Reditum, to drag him through the muck of his past horrors? To let Nalia perform more of her dark rituals on his feeble body?

Halvard sat down at a lonely window seat and stared at the forest below him. His mind rushed. His head hurt. He could feel that familiar trickling, thick liquidy shadow bubbling up from inside his ears. This curse had come back to taunt him. Now, as everything began to spiral with so many disappearances, Halvard found himself wishing that he were dead, that Nalia would have taken his life on that horrible night filled with screaming and pain, spears of shadows being thrust into his mind and heart! The night when the shadows from the wicked woman's hands constricted his young and fragile frame, violating all human senses. His head and chest throbbed as he felt the phantom pain of both creeping back into his memory. Tears welled into his eyes as he recalled. His lips quivered. And now, after 30 years of forcing the curse back, escaping it all, he found himself living that primal fear all over again.

 My brother's mind returned to the matter at hand, conjuring up vast conspiracies. He racked his brain for every possible scenario in which this could have happened. He thought through the people living in his home, the servants, his family, Violet, Sullivan, Shandar, Charles, Isabelle, Agatha, Romilla, Mary! What could have brought all this back? Who summoned that inhuman beast?

 Like a brick falling from the sky and landing on his head, Halvard realized. None of this had happened until the attack in the streets of the city. None of his curse showed itself, not for years, until the police found the girl. The native girl. The one born in the woods, in the snow. It was no wonder she'd looked so familiar to Halvard upon seeing those eyes, that face, that *act* at the funeral.

 "Sent to threaten me and my family," he murmured, wiping away the tears that collected on his cheeks. Of course. It all only fit together, did it not? A native girl mysteriously appears when a native witch decides she needs help with her horrid witchcraft. Decides she needs Halvard. A native girl that looks far too familiar. A native, one of that shadow tribe, would know how to summon such a demon.

 A rage began to form. A rage, my friends, that this man, Halvard Vrana, had never felt in all of his life. Something in his mind felt as though it shattered and leaked, leaked that inky black from his ears. Halvard did nothing to stop it.

 Romilla, Halvard repeated in his mind over and over,

getting up slowly from the window seat. *That girl is no innocent little thing. She's been sent by that devil woman.*

⌘

"Fine time for you to return from your brooding," an angry Violet snapped at her husband, who descended down the stairs. "The police have just gone. Why did you run off like that?"

"Needed to clear my head, dear," Halvard said slowly. His wife didn't catch on to his strange new tone of voice. "You know how I must from time to time."

"Because of your little tantrum, the police are suspicious of you!" the woman whispered, pulling him by his arm. "Have you any idea how much trouble you've gotten us into?" Halvard shook his head like a child being scolded by his mother.

"I...me?" he replied, his voice devoid of emotion. "How dare they think that this mystery nonsense could possibly have been caused by me."

Violet shut the door to the study as she yanked him into it, shooing away the maid sweeping the floor.

"Yes, you!" she said, louder this time. "They think it was you! They want you in for questioning tonight!"

"I...I'm not going," the man mumbled. "Must stay here and protect my family."

Of course, my friends, he couldn't relay the reason. How does one such distraught man hide such a ridiculous secret despite its relevance? And why? For his dignity, perhaps. His sanity. Trust from his loved ones. I couldn't tell you for certain.

"Halvard," Violet pleaded, "I beg of you to go to them, talk some sense into the judges, to prove you're not...that there's nothing to do with you being the cause of this."

"I'm not!" Halvard suddenly yelled. "Why would I ever be the cause of something so monumentally brutal?!"

He pulled his long hair over the side of his face to cover up the black liquid that frothed from his ear.

"Y-yes, Halvard, that's what I mean," Violet said in an attempt to soften up her husband in that moment. "Please be respectful of them, they've been linking a lot of activity to our very household. You must try to-"

"Activity? What do you mean?"

"Two disappearances happened here, one of which we found blood but no...no body."

Halvard looked at his wife's dear face. It was begging with him, pleading for some sense in the world around them. He felt, in that moment, an emotion other than anger - guilt. Guilt for leaving his wife to deal with these matters. Guilt for upsetting the woman he'd loved for decades. And the heavy guttural weight of the consequences he faced.

"I'm sorry, Violet," he said meekly, sitting in the armchair.

"Oh, darling..." Violet took the man's shoulder in her hand and pulled his chin up. She got down to her husband's level and tenderly kissed him on his forehead. "I know we've all been troubled by these events, we've all been suffering through the death of Lizabet and the disappearance of Nancy. But we must face them. I'll come with you to the court tonight."

"No," Halvard mumbled in defeat. "I'll go with Charles. You stay here and watch over the maids and the servants, and Sullivan especially. See that absolutely nothing happens. Keep a close eye on all of them, see to it that no one enters a room alone. I can't afford to lose anyone else."

"Of course, love," Violet answered, embracing her husband. As she pressed her face up against the shoulder of his sleeve, she felt something warm drip onto her head. That motherly instinct overwhelmed her. "Please don't cry, my dear, it'll be all right in the end, you'll see." She kissed the strangely dark tears from his face, not realizing.

"My father was in terrible danger in these woods," my young nephew said as I paced back and forth, drinking sherry from my flask. The boy waved a slip of paper at me. "This writing is nothing short of horrific! He was truly afraid of the woods, for good reason. Wrote about pains in his ears and chest, as though...as though he were inflicted with disease or fragility. Read this yourself, uncle!"

The way that the boy so innocently diverted his attention away from the incredibly pressing matters left me astounded. I took a swig from the flask, feeling my mind starting to go the slightest bit fuzzy.

"Or perhaps he wanted to make up his own legends," I said, only half annoyed. "My dear nephew, have you not noticed that there's a world outside of that little book? One that's crumbling around us now? In this very household?"

The boy shut the book and laid down in his bed.

"I have, uncle. I...I find it difficult to think of. I must distract myself with this new fascination or else I fear I'll go mad. And this is my father! Surely you care about that?"

"What is it about fairy tales and myths that fascinates you so much, then, my dear nephew?" I asked, sitting down on the end off the bed. "I thought you considered yourself to be a grown man, not a naive little boy."

"Surely a young boy didn't write this Compendium," my nephew answered without looking up from the book, a hint of defense creeping into his voice. "There must be other...other men and women interested in these stories, surely."

What a weak argument. Poor boy's head filled with delusions and fantasies. How little like his father he seemed to be! Unless, of course, the childish interest in the forest carried down from father to son.

"I'd imagine you inherited such interest from your father, then," I thought aloud. Sullivan nodded.

"I questioned him about the Reditum, you know," he

said.

"Do tell?"

The boy growled in annoyance when he remembered the dissatisfaction his father provided him with.

"He claimed to be completely uninterested in the woods. Said it like this book never even was his. That's why I wondered if he was frightened of these things. And I read this note and realized he must have hid it away, it even says here!"

"Well, I suppose that wouldn't surprise me," I answered. "After all, he hadn't spoken up about much of anything for months after he'd come home."

"Then why hide that story from me?" Sullivan asked. "Why hide all these fantastic legends?"

I shrugged. Frankly, as much as I loved my dear nephew, I couldn't concentrate on his fantasies. My mind wandered elsewhere as I got back up and paced around his room, deciding to light a cigarette.

A knock at the door prompted the boy to stuff the book under his covers, a routine that he'd gotten very much used to in the past days.

"Yes?" he and I both said in response. Romilla poked her small and cheerful head through the doorway.

"Miss Violet asked that I give you this," she said, handing a lesson-book to the boy. He grimaced. "Said it's necessary for your next study."

"I thought you were a kitchen maid, dear?" he asked, setting the book aside.

"She's got more duties now, of course," I said, matter-of-factly. "As I said, have you not been paying attention to the disappearances of your own servants?" The boy fell silent for a moment. I approached the other side of his bed. "Mm, that's precisely what I'd thought."

"Ah, will there be anything else, masters?" the girl stuttered, nervous at the awkward break. I began to answer with a "no", but Sullivan cut me off.

"Actually, Romilla," he said, pulling his legs over

the edge of the bed, facing her, "Would you stay here for just another moment?"

I saw the boy reach under the covers. I raised my eyebrows.

"What else would you like?" Romilla asked. Sullivan patted the covers of the bed in front of him. Romilla cautiously sat down.

"I'd like to talk," he said. "Surely you're in need of someone to speak to?" I let out a snort.

"I suppose I'll let you two be," I said, getting up from my seat. Sullivan took me by the sleeve.

"No, Uncle Shandar, I want you here too," he said. "I think you're just as curious as I am about certain...happenings." He lifted the book from under the covers, showing Romilla. "Do you know what this is?" he asked.

"I...I can't say I do, sir, no," she said. "What is it?"

"This is a book about everything rumored to be in the Reditum forest," he explained, flipping through the pages very quickly. "I wanted to see if you could...maybe tell us if some of these are true?"

I shook my head and snatched the book from my nephew.

"Uncle-!"

"Would you be reasonable, Sullivan?" I scolded. "Think sensibly! How do you know that Romilla would believe any of this childish rubbish? Why drag her into this?"

"At least let me ask!" he protested. "She's from the Reditum!"

Hesitantly, I returned the book to my nephew and looked at a now fearful Romilla. Oh, how I would have hated to admit that I myself wanted some answers as well. Perhaps my nephew was getting into my head. She sat up straight, rigid with tension. I shivered.

"Apologies for my nephew's childishness," I said sweetly. "He's a young fool."

"I..." Romilla's eyes were brimming with nervous tears. "That's quite all right."

"There's legends all around our area," Sullivan explained to the maid, "of witches and creatures and horrible magic that lurks in the woods. I wondered if there's truth behind it all."

"Talk some sense into him," I said with bitterness, putting my first cigarette into my nephew's ashtray and lighting up a second to ease my nerves. "My nephew is delusional, just like his father before him. He's letting these silly stories get the best of him."

We both looked at Romilla expectantly. To our shock, she stared at her hands, which she wrung together with great force. I could see tears starting to form on her lashes. Sullivan, as curious and as inconsiderate as a boy his age could get, pressed on with the questions.

"Do you remember now what attacked you in the city?" he asked. "Was it a wolf? Or was it something more, something bigger, or horrid?"

"Sullivan!" I hissed. "That's enough, for heaven's sake, look at the poor thing!" Romilla sat there, immobile, afraid that making a single movement would warrant a punishment for not following orders. She pursed her lips and attempted to speak through her now thicker accent.

"It was...neither man nor beast," she said simply. "I don't know what it was."

"Well, never mind that then," I rushed to say before Sullivan could say anything. "Tell us instead about the creatures in the woods that clearly *don't* exist. Prove to him that he's being completely irrational."

I derived a bit of pleasure from seeing my nephew glare at me. Reminded me of old times, of my days watching his father doing the same after a remark I'd just made.

After Romilla wrung her fingers for a few more moments and said nothing in reply to my comment, my smug smirk began to slowly disappear as I felt a twinge of doubt. "Romilla?"

She shook her head.

"There's...there's witches," she replied as though she were being interrogated. "Witches and horrible creatures and horrible, horrible magic."

Sullivan and I stared at her. Surely she wouldn't lie? Perhaps the girl entertained the same fantasies?

"Tell us the truth, Romilla," I said sternly. "Do not lie to the masters of the house."

"She's not, uncle," Sullivan said with a look of awe. "Please, Romilla, can you tell us more? Did you know my father to visit the woods?"

"I...no, sir."

I let out a scoff.

"Even if these silly things were true, she's far too young to have known your father in the past," I said. Alas, it was too late to reason at all with my nephew. Sullivan's wild theories, at least within his own imagination, had - to an extent - been confirmed, by one of the forest, no less. His tone of voice had changed from serious to completely mystified. "Let the poor girl alone, Sullivan, can't you see you've made her cry?" I said, attempting to grab the book back from him. "Of all the people to ask -"

"No, please don't shout," the girl nearly whispered as she stood up, eagerly anticipating the end of the questioning. "Will there be anything else, masters Sullivan and Shandar?"

"Wait, one more thing!" Sullivan said. He opened up the book to the last page, to the note that read, *Thank you, Jura.* He pointed at it and held it up for Romilla to see. "Do you know who Jura is, Romilla?"

Now, I'd seen Romilla cry lightly, before, but the look in her eyes proved to be overwhelmed with emotion. The maid let out a heaving sob and brought her hand to her mouth, stifling the noise. Very suddenly, I felt a gust of cold wind. I jolted as the curtains on the windows blew violently with the sudden change. Sullivan jumped up to close the window to prevent the snow from coming in.

"Bloody hell, it's cold," I shouted over the sound of the slamming window. "Romilla, are you all right?"

Romilla had left the room. Her footsteps pounded against the carpeted stone floor in the hallway.

"Romilla, wait! I'm sorry!"

As my nephew went to chase after her, I stuck my foot out. I'd had enough of his little stories and fantasies, and now he'd gone and made Romilla cry, above it all. The girl needed no more questioning. My nephew tumbled over my outstretched leg and in front of the doorway.

"Bastard!" he called to me as he pulled himself up from the floor, stopping midway.

"I think that's enough of your fairy tales for one night, and perhaps for good," I snapped at him. "Scrape up that stupid book and put it away, where it belongs - in the library." Sullivan ran his fingers along the floor where he'd fallen. "Sullivan, will you listen to me?"

He looked up at me, his dirty blond hair falling out of the ribbon that held it up previously. He pointed to the floor.

"It's ice."

"Stop that, Sullivan. Go to bed at once, before I bring this up with your father."

"Feel it for yourself!" the boy cried. I pursed my lips and muttered obscenities before I felt the floor.

God be damned, he was right. The floor where Romilla was standing before she left was slick and freezing cold to the touch, and crystallized like frost on a window.

"Remarkable," Sullivan murmured. "What do you suppose it is?"

"Just the wind, or...the snow that blew in." I said, hardly believing my own words. "Get to bed now, boy."

What sort of things one will deny, my friends, at least at first, in the midst of tragedy and grief. I left my nephew alone in the room, so that we could both quite stressfully reflect on the mystery of the maid, Romilla.

Chapter 13

Sullivan and I, agreeing that we wanted no more of the curious happenings, decided to go into the city that night. Violet, naturally, became worried at our choice, but I assured her that her son and I would be perfectly safe. At first, she was having none of it, as I expected. Quite frankly, I'd hoped to sneak out without her noticing.

"Please, Violet, let me take the boy into Asterbury," I persisted, my voice carrying heavy annoyance, "It would do him well to get some fresh air."

"Yes mother, let us go," Sullivan whined, rather unprofessionally in comparison to my own firm demand. Speaking to women was not the boy's strong suit, I'd learned quickly.

"Your father instructed me to keep an eye on you, tonight, while he's in court," Violet urged, grabbing her son's shoulder. "Please, stay here for him. For me."

"For heaven's sake, woman, he'll be just fine under my care," I said, sliding my brown greatcoat over my shoulders.

"I'd be fine on my own," Sullivan said, throwing a glare in my direction.

"Regardless, Violet, we're going," I said after sliding on my snow-boots. "If you need to tell your happy husband that his devil of a brother stole away your son for the evening, then so be it. Heaven knows I certainly won't mind."

I clambered into the carriage while Violet stood in the doorway, showering her son with kisses and various "take cares" and "please stay out of harm's way". I felt a twinge of guilt, but I'd soon be drowning that out anyway. Violet's change in attitude when the strange disappearances started happening left me rather surprised - she was normally such a stern figure, like her husband. Once Sullivan finally managed to get himself into the carriage, we sat in a tense silence as it took off and rattled along the cobbled roads. I could tell by my nephew's own tense demeanor that he wanted to drown his own sorrows out with drink as well. Like his, I'm sure, my mind kept returning to Romilla as I heard the moody whistling of the wind and saw the snowflakes gently pattering against the coach.

When we arrived at our destination, a small pub of my choosing (very merry little place, I'd hoped to get my spirits up there), Sullivan and I sat down at the bar, calling for a few drinks.

"Apologies for my behavior earlier," I said to my nephew, "I hope you weren't hurt after you fell."

"While I didn't appreciate it, I'm not hurt," the boy replied after downing a pint. "I accept your apology, but I hope that you see now what I've been trying to say."

I hesitated. Of course, I'd seen with my own eyes, felt with my own hands what appeared to be some type of cold witchcraft. Whether or not my mind's logic dared to believe my senses seemed impossible to figure.

"I'm still comprehending," I answered simply. "I thought myself to be a rational man, and now I fear I'm not."

"How can you rationalize such an occurrence?" my nephew asked, his voice low. "There's no other possible explanation except that Romilla is..."

"Yes, yes, yes," I said, waving a hand at him, afraid someone might hear. "Is there a chance you'll let this subject rest, at least for this evening?"

"Not if there's a connection between this and the murders," the boy whispered, leaning in closer to me. "My theory is that whatever creature it was that attacked Romilla, attacked the other maids, only they didn't make it out alive. Highly relevant to the matters at hand."

"If you're so convinced, then you may bring it up to the police," I snapped. "That book's getting to your head and you know it."

The boy went quiet. It wasn't very often, after all, that we'd quarrel. The more he persisted on bringing up something that seemed so beyond reason, the more I became irate. Could I give you a reason why? Perhaps I'd been too preoccupied with the difficulties the household went through. These randomly targeted murders were no childish matter, and that's what Sullivan was to me - a child. A curious and easily fascinated boy. The more he attempted to intertwine the readings in a silly fairy tale book with the grave depravities, the more I felt my senses as an adult, a grown-up, being ignored. Perhaps I found myself searching for that same validation that my nephew coveted - to be seen as a grown person and not a child. However, as much as I tried to teach him the ways and manners of a young man, I couldn't escape his constant youthful naivety.

    We sat in silence for a few more moments, listening to the cheerful chatter of the other patrons in the bar. Sullivan managed to get through yet another pint in that short time, the little fool. I called for another drink, and the bartender obliged.

    "You hear the rumors?" he asked as he set the glass in front of me. I nodded.

    "I'm almost too aware," I replied coldly. Despite my demeanor and curt reply, the man continued on.

    "Word around here is that the esteemed Halvard Vrana is linked to the disappearances," he said. Sullivan and I jolted at the mention of the name.

    "And why would anyone believe that?" I asked, before kicking my nephew so he wouldn't say a word about it.

    "If you think about it, two of 'em happened in his house, and I heard he left the scene of the crime unscathed and without the maid that vanished. If you ask me, I'd say he's the one doin' all this."

    "I don't know if I believe that," Sullivan piped up. I only pursed my lips and stared straight down at the countertop. I prayed to all that was holy that he didn't mention that book. "I...I heard that Mister Vrana was too distressed about it all to have done anything wrong."

    "He could have been putting on an act, you know,"

the barkeep said, amused. "Anyway, Who are you to be speaking on such matters, hm?"

"I'm-oh!"

I knocked the boy on the back, causing him to spill his third drink everywhere. I couldn't have him revealing that he was an alleged murderer's son, now could I? The man behind the counter laughed.

"As I thought, you're a mere boy who's had one too many of those," he chortled. "Want a glass of milk, young man?"

"For god's sake, will nobody stop calling me a boy?!" my nephew yelled, slamming his hands on the bar. "Get me five more of those, and we'll see who's the boy!"

"Sullivan-" I started, but never finished.

"No! I won't stop until everyone else stops!" he said. "I'm tired of it all! Tired of it! I'm eighteen, I'm studying my father's work! I've had my share of drinks and pleasured many women!"

"Get a grip, nephew!" I ordered, grabbing the boy's arm. "Good god, you're already drunk!"

"I'll say what I want to, uncle, and you're not going to hold me back! You're just the same as mother and father!" he cried, standing on the counter. I attempted to pull at him, but he kicked my hands away, then kicked away the barkeep. The patrons looked at him, some with amusement, others with fear. "If I hear one more comment about being a boy, god help you! All of you!" he shouted. I'll admit, the boldness impressed me by the slightest.

"That is *enough*!" I hissed. "Get down this instant, or I'll-"

"You'll see! That's what you'll get for trifling with Sullivan Vrana!!"

All that was left of that little speech was the sound of my dear nephew breathing heavily. By god, you could hear a pin drop in the rest of the pub as everyone stared in our direction.

"Vrana?" the barkeep said, his voice strangely quiet.

"In relation to Halvard Vrana?"

"Not at all, not at all," I stammered, my eyes darting back and forth between Sullivan and the barkeep. "Not a clue who that is."

"You and the boy look like him," chimed a woman sitting along the wall. "Is he not Halvard's son?"

"And not a boy!" Sullivan cried. The barkeep swept his large arm underneath my nephew's legs, causing him to come crashing down, slamming his head on the wooden counter. I attempted to catch him as he slid off the front, moaning in pain. The entirety of the room laughed. "Bastard..." he mumbled, before he fainted as dead weight in my arm's grip. I struggled to pull his arm over my shoulder.

"Get out of my pub," the barkeep hissed at us. "You expect me to run a respectable business with you and him around?"

"I assure you, this is a large misunderstanding," I grumbled. I could hardly keep anything a secret now that my nephew had brought up the one thing he shouldn't have. I pulled him towards the door whilst a large amount of the others either stared at us or laughed at us. This boy had done nothing but make me a laughing stock as of late. And I'm not so sure how much longer I could have tolerated it.

"Uncle, tell that insufferable bastard..." Sullivan muttered, his voice fading into something unintelligible as he stirred. I dragged him to the carriage. Just as the coachman and I began guiding him inside, I noticed he had started bleeding from the side of his face.

"Damn it all, boy," I whispered, my rage building. I pulled out a handkerchief from my front pocket and wiped away the blood. Another carriage pulled up behind ours. I paid it no mind until I heard the shouting.

"Shandar, you idiot, what have you done?!"

Halvard's voice. There was no getting out of this one, I'm afraid.

"Boy hit his head," I murmured as my brother stormed towards us, his finest cloak blowing behind him in the freezing wind. "Slipped on some ice."

"Father, tell them all I'm not a boy anymore!" Sullivan cried drunkenly. We both ignored him.

"Why did you bring him here?" Halvard demanded, yanking me away and inspecting his son's face. "I gave strict orders to stay at home!" For once, I couldn't come up with anything clever to say. Rather, I felt myself growing irritable at both my brother and his son.

"To be frank, I'm not so sure why I brought your little brat here," I replied, my own voice rising. "I thought he'd be good company, all he's been is trouble! That's all he ever is!"

"Don't you insult my son, Shandar!" Halvard roared after tending to Sullivan's wound, pointing a finger at me. "It's you who's brought this disgusting lifestyle into his world! You who's ruined him!"

"And it's you, his own father, who would never pay him attention the way I do!" I cried. "I don't see you interfering in his life to teach him a damned thing! You skitter away on your little joy walks! At least I pay the boy mind, like a true father!"

"I've taught him more than you ever will, and you know it!"

"If it wasn't for me, your son would be miserable!"

"My son would have been better off and less of a little fool if not for you!"

This made me see red, of course. I could only manage one word.

"Liar!"

"Degenerate!"

A powerful blow landed against the side of my face, knocking me completely off-balance. In the moments I fell to my knees, I heard Sullivan's muffled shouting and some shocked reactions from the small crowd around us. Halvard began barking orders. "Don't help him, Charles! Sullivan, you stay in the carriage! Shandar, I forbid you from coming back home tonight! Stay here where you belong, crawling through the muck at the bottom of the city with the rest of the rats!"

I hoisted myself back up from the snowy cobblestone. My eyes stung for the first time in years. In that moment of my heaving chest, my fight against tears, I felt that genuine, horrible, dreadful feeling of guilt creeping up into my throat. He was right. Sullivan was the way he was all because of his uncle. Because of me.

"I'm sorry, Halvard."

"Only sorry because you won't have a place to stay tonight," my little brother sneered. He got very close to my face, taking my collar in his hands. "If I see you snooping around my home tonight, then you will be severely punished, is that clear?"

As I was about to nod sheepishly, my mind's eye conjured up a disturbing image - a vision of a shadowy figure with two strong hands around my neck. I blinked. In my brother's aging eyes, I saw...nothing. Just black. I yanked his hands away from me.

"Your...your eyes-"

The eyes went back to their normal color after he closed them tightly and opened them back up. He growled.

"Charles, follow Thomas' coach back home,"

Halvard said, stepping quickly away from me and into the carriage. I stood against the brick wall of the pub and watched the carriages leave. I caught a glimpse of Sullivan wiping his eyes and nose - he was crying. My mind went back to the image I'd seen. I thought the unthinkable. Quite suddenly I became as rational as the city folk, believing, if only for a moment, that my brother was truly going mad, taking out his fits of anger on others, little by little. After the things I'd seen that day spun round and round in my head, I wandered the streets for another pub to drink my them away.

※

Sullivan awoke the next morning with a start. Sweat shimmered on his brow and above his upper lip. The boy always found himself waking up from horrible nightmares after those nights out in the city with his uncle - caused by the drink, no doubt. He looked at the window to discover that morning had indeed broken.

"Sullivan, dear?" Violet stood at the foot of his bed, a look of fatigued concern etched on her face. The boy jolted upon hearing her voice.

"Good morning, mother," he replied groggily, realizing as he sat up just how much his head hurt. He felt his cheek, where a small plaster bandage had been applied to his wound from the night before. "Where's Uncle Shandar?"

"Not a word about him," Violet scolded immediately as she opened the drapes. "Your father was rather angry about it last night. Forbade your uncle from returning with you. I did warn you to stay home."

The boy rubbed at his eyes and laid back down.
"I feel ill."

"Well, after what your father told me last night, I'd imagine you do," the woman said,
placing a hand over his forehead. "I'll send someone up with tea and breakfast, my darling. I need to keep a close eye on your father today."

"Why?"

Violet let out a long sigh. She sat on the side of Sullivan's bed.

"Charles mentioned that he lost his temper with the judges last night," she whispered. "I fear that more of these outbursts are imminent, he's not taking too kindly to the horrid things that have been happening. At least, one can only hope that's why he's acting in such a way."

Sullivan nodded slowly.
"What did the judges say?"

"All I know is that they weren't happy," Violet replied, tears brimming in her eyes. "I...I don't know what's happening to him. He's never gotten so angry before. Never lost his temper quite so easily."

Through his aching stomach and head, the curiosity continued to burn.

"Did...did anything happen to him? When he was young?" the boy asked. Violet looked at her son, concerned.

"The worst happening that I know of was his encounter with the Reditum," she answered hesitantly. "Got lost, but returned home. His mother claimed that he kept very quiet for a long time, but I saw him as normal. Merely thoughtful and stern. He seemed fine after he grew up." The two sat in silence for a moment, before Violet stood up and cleared her throat. "As I said, my dear, I must go keep him in bed today. I'll send someone up for you directly."

"Yes, mother."

Violet went from the room, a nervous hen of what she used to be. Sullivan covered his eyes with his hand to block the light from them and stop the pain in his head. It seemed the entire household was falling apart, everyone was on edge, nobody listened to him. Even his uncle Shandar, the one whom he'd grown so fond of, claimed that he was nothing but trouble. Everything truly was crumbling around him, everyone acted so differently. What strange times these were! In order to silence these wretched thoughts, the boy reached for the little purple book under the pillow. He opened to the page he'd left off on when a maid knocked at the door.

"Yes?"

"Breakfast and tea, Master Sullivan," came a timid voice from behind the door. Sullivan felt a chilly breeze brush past his neck.

"Come in, Romilla."

Romilla opened the door with a small cart of tea, sausages, and toast.

"Miss Violet said you weren't feeling well, so she asked me to bring you whatever you need today," the girl said, pouring the tea into a cup. Sullivan nodded.

"Very good," he mumbled, catching himself staring

at the floor beneath the girl's feet. He looked back up, where Romilla placed a tray on the side table.

"And how are you today, master Sullivan?" she asked, reciting the lines she'd been taught.

"Feeling ill, and a case of the morbs," he replied.

"Ah, peppermint tea, my favorite, you know," Sullivan said.

"Miss Agatha said so," Romilla answered. "Said it would have you feeling better in no time at all."

"Mm." There was a pause while Romilla carefully set up the tray. Sullivan attempted a passing, subtle comment. "I feel that you know more about me than I'll ever know about you, dear," the boy said. Romilla didn't dare look up from her work, carefully stacking dishes on the cart.

"With...with all due respect, master, I should like to keep it that way."

Sullivan pursed his lips. Through his headache and his sadness, he still managed to dig up that curiosity. Perhaps he felt it was the only escape from the world around him: to learn new things of perhaps mystical nature. Things that stood directly in front of him - a mystery to be solved.

"Come now, we both know what happened yesterday," he whispered. Romilla, being the obedient little creature she was, turned her attention to the young master of the house.

"I can't say I do, sir," the girl mumbled. Sullivan brought her hands into his. Of course, her hands were cold, even after pouring the piping hot tea.

"Oh, but you do," he said. "Romilla, there was ice on the ground, right where you stood. You can't deny what I'd seen, what I felt." The girl hung her head. "Please, please don't cry," Sullivan said gently. "Tell me, Romilla, surely you're hiding something. It can't do you any good to keep it all inside." Romilla pulled her hands away from Sullivan only to have her arm gingerly grabbed instead. "Where are you from, Romilla? Who are you, really?"

Poor Romilla attempted to keep the tears from falling. Her timidity couldn't have gotten her away this time.

With the only courage she felt she could muster, Romilla spoke up.

"I am...cursed," she said. Sullivan crinkled his brow.

"Cursed?"

Romilla nodded.

"Please don't tell anyone, please, mister Sullivan."

"Oh, Romilla, I won't tell a soul," he said with an earnest sincerity. "How did it happen?"

"Born with it," she continued, "Everyone except mother hated me. Grandmother especially. She frightened me." Sullivan grasped on to every word. Suddenly he started to realize why the girl always cried. "She couldn't take it anymore, said I was...was a blasphemer. She tried to have me..."

My nephew looked at the girl intently, then remembered her lying motionless on the city street.

"Killed?" he asked softly.

"Yes," Romilla uttered, rubbing tears off from her cheeks. "Mother...mother couldn't protect me. She died trying."

Sullivan let go of the girl's arm suddenly, as it became very cold, even through the dress sleeve. He stood up from his bed as tears dribbled down the sides of the maid's face, freezing in mid-air and clinking as they hit the floor. His urge to question her further started to fade. He'd upset her yet again. Curiously enough, however, Romilla chose to continue.

"Jura," she whispered. "Jura was my mother."

Sullivan nodded and reflected. Unusual. His father met Romilla's mother. Given the constant doting from his own parents, the boy had a difficult time imagining something so hideously vile.

"Why would your own family member want you dead?" he mumbled.

"I...I was not born of the shadows like my grandmother." Romilla buried her face in her apron.

"Oh, Romilla, dry your eyes, dear," Sullivan said.

"I'm so sorry for making you uncomfortable again."

"I am the one with the curse," the girl sobbed. "And yet you're being so kind to me. Do I not frighten or disgust?"

Sullivan shook his head.

"You've never frightened or disgusted me," he said. "On the contrary, I'm fascinated by you. You're...you're quite a mystery. Rather unexpected."

Ah, how the mind of the young works. Anyone else might have been truly terrified of Romilla's unnatural abilities. Oh, but how lucky she was to have met a wide-eyed and curious young man, one of whom believed in such magic despite the words of others. And now, he not only believed in the strange abilities, but he knew of them.

"I suppose...I suppose someone should know," Romilla said, wiping her eyes and nose. "About my past."

"I'm happy to lend an ear. But I do have one more question..."

"Hm?"

Sullivan opened up the little compendium and pointed to the note regarding Romilla's mother.

"Did your mother ever tell you about my father? He was lost in the Reditum once as a boy, I can only assume that he encountered your...your tribe, or perhaps just your mother based on this note."

"I...I can't say for sure," the maid replied, "but my grandmother oft spoke of her 'shadow prince'. She went mad whenever she spoke of his escape. Violent outbursts...told me he was destined for great things, while I was...was a stain upon her life."

Sullivan noticed tears again. He quickly tried to quell them.

"Well, there's no need to tell me anything else," Sullivan said. "You're already sad just remembering. I don't want you to face the cheery Agatha with tears in your eyes. So, you are dismissed."

"You...You don't need anything else?"

"No, dear, nothing," the boy said. "I only ask that

you keep your chin up. You're safe from all that now."

Romilla nodded as she took hold of the tea cart. She looked back for a moment at Sullivan.

"Thank you, mister Sullivan," she whispered. "Bless you."

"Enough of that 'master' business," my nephew said, a smile shining through, "You have permission to call me 'Sullivan'."

"Thank you," the girl said. The wind came through the window, bringing a gentle breeze into the room. "Oh, thank you."

⁂

"Where is he?!"

Petimus' body shriveled and wrinkled as it twisted back, avoiding the woman's arm as she took a swing at the creature.

"I'm taking his s-servants," Petimus stammered. "One at a time. City dwellers too. Me and Verdorben have been dreadfully hungry-"

"Servants! Servants!" Nalia shrieked, throwing both a stool and a book at Petimus, both successfully striking him and raising instant bruises on his deadened skin. "Servants mean nothing to me! Nothing! I need my king! Where is he?!"

"He's...he's attacked me," Petimus whimpered hideously. "I cannot bring him on my own. Too powerful. Too angry."

"Then take what he loves," Nalia hissed, grabbing the thing by its neck and shaking him. "Loved ones! That's where the weakness is! Fool! Disgrace!"

Nalia released Petimus, who dropped to the ground with a loud cracking sound. His neck where the woman held him was now black with both bruises and the woman's shadows.

"I-I'm sorry," he said, hoisting himself up with

broken joints and snapping them back into place. "I've displeased my mistress, my mother of the shadows."

"Sorry?" Nalia hissed. "You haven't seen sorry. Not yet."

Nalia snapped her fingers at a shadow next to her table. Verdorben rose from the ground, then immediately stepped back upon seeing the suddenly calm witch towering over him. Nalia started to stroke his head.

"I've grown fond of you both," the woman cooed. "The legends say you're always together. As I made you." She put a hand on Verdorben's back as she continued to pet him.

"A-always and forevermore, like our loyalty to you, our creator," Petimus replied nervously, stepping closer to his pet. Nalia shoved him away.

"Hmm." Nalia sat the corpse of the canine beast down, speaking softly to him and scratching under his chin. Her other hand found its way to Verdorben's long chest. Verdorben let out a sudden yelp of pain and thrashed violently as a pointed javelin of black pierced from the witch's hand and through the beast's back. Petimus looked away, unable to close his bulging eyes. The beast fell on its side with a dull thud.

"Verdorben..." Petimus said, the slightest tinge of hurt creeping into his hissing voice. "Me pup..."

He looked over to see the body of his former pet, collapsed and deflating, releasing all that had been keeping it alive like black smoke. The bones and skin dissolved into dust that scattered at Nalia's feet. Petimus approached the dust and picked it up, letting it run through his bony fingers.

"Now do you see what I mean?" Nalia asked harshly. "Do as I say. Find his loved ones. Take them. Lure him. My king, my leader of the shadow army. Or you'll be next."

Petimus sank into the floor, unable to cry or mourn.

Chapter 14

  I recall wandering into my brother's home as quietly as possible the next morning. Of course, it wasn't the first time I'd sauntered in after a long night, though this time I felt much less satisfaction as I hung my furs in the front hall and attempted to avoid the eyes of the servants, or my own family. I shut myself into my room, praying that my dear young nephew wouldn't dare come visit. I despised the idea of having to face him. I despised that I would eventually have to face my brother, the one who'd been acting so strangely over the past weeks. Not a single thought of joy or merriment ran through my mind after what had happened. Not a scrap of light fell into the workings of my mind, the feelings within my heart - all were overtaken by a shadow of horrible dread, guilt, and gloom that galloped around and spread lies like crops in the frozen field of my emotion. Therefore, I'd opted to stay within the room and not speak a word to anyone - I felt, that morning, like my moody brother.

  In another part of the house, Violet sat in her chair, providing lists of tasks for the staff and keeping the books, the usual morning hustle and bustle. Halvard approached the doorway, looking particularly disheveled.

  "Haven't you slept yet, darling?" Violet asked as she took a glance at him and continued with her work.

  "Hardly," was the response. "I must speak with you. Urgently."

  The woman raised an eyebrow and shooed the few maids out of the room. Halvard closed the door behind him.

  "What's this about?" Violet said. Halvard paced in front of his wife, a nervous wreck of a man.

  "My darling, I've been up for the whole of the night reflecting on this," he said, with the slightest tremble in his voice. "You must listen to me, as I fear not many others would."

  "I'm listening, dear," Violet replied after a moment's hesitation. "What's gotten you so worried?"

"It...it has come to my attention that there may be suspicious activity happening within this home, and I'm not going to tolerate it."

Violet felt a horrible dread rise into her throat and claw at it.

"What do you mean?" she asked.

"There's evidence of these attacks only occurring with someone in particular present."

Violet furrowed her brow and put down her ink pen. She chewed her lip nervously. Surely her husband wasn't speaking about himself?

"Are you talking about the judges, Halvard, and what they mentioned?"

"I'm talking about Romilla."

What a shock Violet felt as he said the girl's name. She shook her head in complete and utter disbelief. She felt the need to choose her words very carefully.

"Darling, I...whatever made you come to such a conclusion?"

"Have you not noticed, Violet?" Halvard whispered, leaning closer to his wife. "This strange girl, found in the streets and brought into society - ever since, there's been attacks, missing people, our own servants!"

"Halvard, the poor girl laid half-dead there for god knows how long, how could she possibly-"

"-have brought someone-something-sinister from her home? From those accursed woods? It's entirely possible, Violet!"

At this point, Violet began to see a gleam of something wild in her husband's eyes, his tired face, his heaving chest. She stood up from her chair and placed a hand on Halvard's cheek.

"I think, my dear, that...that you most certainly need Doctor Howell," she said as calmly as possible. Halvard's eyes widened and he pushed off the woman's gentle hand.

"How can you not see it?" the man hissed, "This girl has brought something upon us here, Violet, it's endangering us all!"

"What on-Halvard, you're not rational! The girl's the most sweet and polite little thing, she'd never hurt a fly!"

"A ruse!" Halvard shouted. "It's all a mind game! She's not the timid little thing she's shown you!"

"Please lower your voice, and stop spitting rubbish!"

"Violet, I would never!"

"You're accusing an innocent child of horrid things, and I won't tolerate it! I'm calling for Doctor Howell, you just aren't well! These outbursts aren't like you!"

Halvard let out a short breath and sank into the chair across from his wife.

"You have to believe that there is good reason behind these outbursts, dear," he replied. Violet came closer to him and knelt down, looking him in the eyes in an attempt to quell her angry husband.

"The murders of so many is disconcerting, for certain," his wife said in the most soothing of voices she could manage. "But this is no reason to be calling out this poor girl. I assure you she's been acting normal since she arrived here. Timid, but quite content and obedient."

"You've no idea!" the man shouted as suddenly as he stood up. Violet stumbled backwards and let out a frightened gasp. "She's lying to all of us! She's brought a figure to pick off the city folk one by one, little by little, striking into my own home!"

Violet-for the first time in her life-felt afraid of this man. Afraid for her own safety. Something had overwhelmed the charming and moody man she'd married. Horrible thoughts and conspiracies now clouded his mind.

"You get back in bed, Halvard," Violet ordered shakily, pointing to the door, "I beg of you. You're not yourself."

"Not myself!" he cried, standing up and knocking books off the side-table. "Not myself! This girl, she's done awful things, I know her type! I'm trying to save you, I'm trying to save Sullivan, I'm trying to rid my home from this scourge, this-this native plague! This has nothing to do with me being myself or not!"

Violet's whole body shook with sobs.

"What's happened to you, darling?"

"Far more than I could ever share now," Halvard responded. He grabbed something from the table. "And for the sake of everyone in this household, I'm getting rid of that girl."

"Halvard, surely you're not-what do you mean?!" Violet ran to her husband and clutched at his shoulders. Halvard glared at her with fiery eyes.

"Do not insinuate, woman," he hissed, "No matter what the people say, you know I'd never harm a soul."

"But, Halvard-"

"I only aim to protect my family from harm, and this is more urgent than you could ever imagine. I am the only one who can keep you safe, and you're not to get in my way."

Halvard took his wife's hands from his shoulders and shoved her aside. The woman tried to step closer but felt something hold her back-her foot caught in a puddle of something terribly sticky and she grabbed the decorative table as she fell forward.

"Halvard!" she shouted too late. Halvard shut the door behind him, and turned the key in the lock. He heard his wife shouting from the room, alone, and felt tears welling up in his eyes. Regardless, he hastily tucked the key in his pocket and quickly walked away from that room, on a mission, looking for the young, native girl.

༄

Agatha stood in the kitchen, humming merrily. It was her job, you see, to keep order among the staff amongst the outrageous events. She made peace with her jolly nature, telling jokes and keeping spirits up when they were so grim for everyone else. The kitchen, as usual, was the happiest place in that home.

As she began pulling dishes from the shelves, the woman heard a dark and gloomy voice call her.

"Agatha, dear."

She turned to see the silhouette of my brother standing in the doorway, both hands tucked away in his trouser pockets. "A moment with Romilla, please."

"Of course, master Halvard. Oh, Romilla!"

The girl looked up from her sweeping as she heard Agatha calling for her.

"Yes, miss?"

"Ah, come 'ere, child, the master'd like to see you!"

Romilla stepped from the pantry into the kitchen, and set her broom aside. She gazed up at the dark man towering over her.

"If you don't mind, Agatha, I'd like to speak with Romilla alone, upstairs. My, er, wife and I have to speak to her."

The rest of the kitchen maids stopped their work for a moment. Agatha nodded.

"Whatever you wish, master. Go on, child, the sweepin' can be done afterwards."

"Yes, miss!"

Oh, such glee in the girl's voice, the girl's young, naive little voice. Halvard felt no sympathy nor endearment as he heard it.

"Follow me, Romilla."

As the two walked away from the kitchen, a few of the maids peeked out into the hall. Mary, the oldest of them, shook her head.

"You remember the last time we left the master alone with one of the girls?" she asked feebly. Agatha knocked the woman on the back.

"Do not bring up that rubbish, Mary," she said, though the words had most definitely crept into her own mind and formed their own theories. "Now someone fetch the breakfast orders from miss Violet, I've not yet heard from her."

Halvard and Romilla walked up the stairs and into Halvard's bedroom. Halvard closed the door behind him and gestured to the armchair by the fireplace. The girl sat down.

"Where's miss Violet?" she asked. "You said she had to speak to me as well?"

"She must be elsewhere," the man mumbled.

"So then, you'd...like to speak with me?" she asked. Halvard let out a grunt.

"I'd like to ask you some questions, certainly."

Now beginning to feel afraid, the girl nodded. What it was that concerned her, she would never have been able to explain. A sort of mild fear, a creeping sensation of dread. Something that created a heavy weight in her mind. Perhaps Sullivan had told his father about what happened? Why it felt so cold in that room? The frost she left behind as she walked?

"Of course," she replied in a feeble voice. "What would you like to ask?"

"You know, it's been rather difficult here without Lizabet and Nancy," he started. "Would you agree?"

"Why...I can't say for sure, I hardly knew them, master."

Halvard grunted again and swiveled around to face the girl.

"What sort of fool do you take me for?" he asked. Understandably, Romilla's jaw went slack. The fear welled up in her chest, much greater than she initially felt.

"I...I don't understand."

"Of course you do," Halvard hissed. "Tell me where you're from?"

"The...the woods," the girl answered nervously. A noticeable draft suddenly formed in the room. Halvard stood over the seat the girl was in and blocked her from getting out. He placed his arms on the arms of the chair and leaned in.

"One of them, then," he whispered, pointing an

accusatory finger at her. "What a mysterious entrance you made, fooling everybody, fooling my own wife, child, and brother!"

"Sir, please-"

"Clever setup for being of the woods," Halvard continued, "Half dead in the city-ha! I know your type, I know who you work for, no need to correct me!"

Halvard took the girl by the collar and forced her out of the chair and onto the floor. Romilla scampered backwards, the dread in her mind quickly becoming an intense fear. Tears pooled in her eyes and rolled down her cheeks. Halvard sneered at the sight.

"Hiding behind tears will not work on me!" he roared. "Hiding behind that timid little disguise! I know what you really are!" The girl held up an arm in a weak attempt to defend herself.

"Please, master, stop!"

"You'll be gaining no pity from me, not after what you've done to my household!"

Halvard's ears dripped with black as he pulled Romilla up by the arm and threw her into the bedpost. Shadows oozed through the man's fingers and he grabbed Romilla by the arm again. The black oozed out and onto Romilla's skin.

"What have you to say for yourself, before I rid this house of your kind forever?"

Romilla sobbed and yanked and tugged her arm to free it, but to no avail. She looked up at her master's eyes – swirling shadows overtook them. She'd seen it one too many times before. The scourge of her life appeared before her again, in those eyes. The one who'd hated her for her entire life, the one who tried to have her killed. She wailed aloud in anguish as her arm grew colder and colder, like frost on glass. Halvard let go, startled. The girl ran for the door, leaving on the wooden bedpost a thick layer of ice. Halvard's rage quickly turned into shock upon the gripping realization. The words of Petimus returned to his mind.

"*...Jura's bastard daughter, born of the cold and not of the shadow.*"

The door opened, revealing a stunned Doctor Howell, Violet Ann, myself, and a few maids. Romilla rushed into the arms of Violet, sobs erupting from her mouth.

"Halvard!" Violet screamed, her voice shrill with horror. "What have you done?!"

"I..." my brother clumsily attempted to explain. "I was-"

"Get Romilla to safety, Mrs. Vrana," Doctor Howell ordered in a stern and urgent tone. "Now. *Now*, do you hear me?"

Violet ran along with Romilla close behind her. The doctor and I stepped into the room, noticed dark drops scattered across the carpet and on his hands. I could scarcely believe what I was seeing.

"Shandar-" I looked at my wild-eyed brother and picked up a book from the shelf, slowly and carefully. "Shandar, I've done nothing, please believe me, please!"

I shook my head before swinging the book at the side of his head with all of my strength. Doctor Howell and I watched as my madman of a brother limply collapsed back into the bed.

Chapter 15

Sullivan flipped through the book, reading each leaflet very carefully. Every page intrigued him, he didn't want to miss a single word or letter after reading his father's frantic note. The book opened a sense of wonder in him, something he'd been trying to find even as he visited the pubs of Asterbury. It made him feel like a young child again, reading of the wonders of the Reditum forest, the one that his father had gotten lost inside and then refused to let his son get anywhere near.

Another page flip revealed a mess of scribbled-out printed text, and beneath it some scrawled handwriting. Sullivan squinted at it, not realizing he'd sat up, his focus more intense. The print was barely legible and faded, nearly impossible to read, save for the title: "The Legend of the Kind Hag". It could only be assumed that the text recited this legend of a kind yet ugly old woman. The slip of paper claimed otherwise.

The handwriting distracted from the order and tidiness of the print. It looked like panicked scrawls and scribbles, like the scratches of an asylum patient, crying out for help.

"*Lies, all of it. Every word, false! No kindness. They're after me. There's only hatred. Beggars and witches and curses! Don't do as it says. Do not return.*" He flipped a page to read over more scribbles. "*My ears hurt! She hurt me so! I bleed ink!*" Disturbed, the boy frowned. He moved his lips as he read over the writing again and again. As long as he'd been alive, his father remained calm, even in the most distressing situations, such as the recent disappearances of the maids.

Noteworthy that he's acted out in front of everyone, he thought.

"*They're after me...beggars and witches and curses.*'

His father never went back into the woods, had they all followed him afterward?

'Don't do as it says. Do not return.'

Were they still after him, after all these years? The beggars and the witches? No. The first strike had happened in the city. Away from his father. To Romilla. Then more targeted city-goers, not his father.

Sullivan flipped back to the poem of the beggar. He'd read it numerous times before, but for the sake of curiosity, he read through it again. His mouth followed the words until he was whispering each one. The image in his mind of such a violent, nearly human creature gave him a thrill. And besides, did it mention anything of vengeance? Did the creature want revenge?

The words dribbled from his lips in soft mumbles.

"*...Don't scream as he seizes, he'll do as he pleases, tearing through you with claws made of lies...*"

Romilla had scars described as claw marks. She survived the perpetrator's attack.

"No, no," Sullivan mumbled, feeling more rational as he thought of his uncle's words. "I'm getting lost in legends." He snapped the book shut, though not before hearing sounds of anguish just down the hall.

⁂

"Let me be! Let go!"

Halvard struggled to break free from the arms of the policemen and the doctor that held him firmly and dragged him towards the stairs. The chief turned to the sobbing wife whilst my brother shouted.

"It's the lock-up for him, I'm afraid," the large man said. "Criminal lunacy is my own suspicion."

Violet let out a wail and put her face in her hands.

"Please, please, no!" she cried. I placed a hand on her shoulder and looked over to my brother, his panicked face, his messy hair - all factors pointed to lunacy, but I couldn't help but have my own doubts. I kept them to myself as the chief continued on.

"Intent to harm may only be a minor offence, but the magistrate might say otherwise. But lunatics often strike again. If you asked me, I'd keep this man out of anyone's contact for some time."

"Oh, he can't be one of them! My husband doesn't belong in an asylum! Please, please at least let me go with him!"

"Too dangerous," the chief said. He addressed me next, seeing how much more composed I was compared to Violet. "Sir, the magistrate will need to see the girl tomorrow."

"Yes, yes," I sighed. "We'll comply in any way needed, officer."

"I should hope so," the man replied. "Take him into the hansom, Lucius."

"Right!"

I watched helplessly. Halvard continued shouting at the officers until he locked his gaze on me and on his wife. Something changed in that moment as his face went from angry and tense to crestfallen and strangely calm.

"Let me speak to my family, please, and say goodbye," he said, defeated. I raised my eyebrows. The sudden mood shift startled me.

"Halvard!" Violet ran towards her husband and threw her arms around him. She held him for a long few moments before they whispered to each other. My own mind spiraled, looking for what could have been the logical explanation for all. I heard footsteps behind me.

"Uncle!" I swiveled around, greeted by my nephew's own panicked expression. I shook my head at him and grabbed him by the arm.

"Do not interfere, Sullivan," I hissed. "I'll explain later. Please, go back to your room at once."

"Let me say goodbye, Shandar!" Halvard ran up the hallway. The police jolted at his sudden movements and came after him. He gripped his son's shoulders in a frenzy. "Sullivan, please take care of your mother while I'm away.

Protect the house. You and your uncle. Please."

Sullivan's eyes grew wide.

"Father, what's happened?" The officers and doctor Howell took Halvard's arms again and pulled him off of his darling, frightened son. As they yanked him away, the boy felt a warm drop on his hand. Blood? Or perhaps "ink"? Halvard fell to his knees and let out a long, labored sigh. He clutched his head. "Father?"

"I...I..."

"Last goodbye, Mr. Vrana," the chief warned. The policemen let go. Halvard stood up again, very slowly. He kept his head down.

"Everyone is to leave this household immediately," he said sternly, through gasping breaths. "Everyone, do you hear me? I want everyone in a safe place! Violet, please!"

The chief grabbed onto Halvard's collar while the other officers swarmed him.

"Sad case, this one," the chief said. "I'm sorry, sonny, but your father has committed assault on a house servant," he pointed at the stairs, "and must be taken immediately before someone else is hurt."

The other officers caught on to the chief's annoyance and quickly began taking my brother away. Halvard fought like a child being restrained. His eyes were wild and his face more gaunt than ever - he screamed and clawed and begged. I clutched at my nephew, in a quick reaction to protect him. Violet did as well, covering her mouth in one hand and gasping as she cried.

"Wait! Wait, please! Stop! Something's wrong!" Halvard shouted, his lungs sounding exhausted with the desperation.

I kept holding Sullivan's arm, watching, waiting for the noise and commotion to end. My throat tightened. How could my brother, the most composed and reserved man, have gone mad in a matter of weeks? Could he really have been like this for so much time, taking the lives of the innocent in his state of horrific insanity?

Before I could continue my musings, I heard the voice of not my brother, but the police.

"Get him! Find him!"

I stared ahead as they ran down the stairs, some tripping on the way.

"Violet, Sullivan," I started, "pack at once and meet me in the front, we need to take shelter in the city tonight. Now."

"But Shandar-"

"*Now!*" I demanded. "We can't afford any more to be lost! Order everyone to remove themselves from here immediately, Violet! Go!"

She scurried off, skirts lifted and face drenched with shiny tears. Sullivan wrenched his way out of my grip that I'd forgotten about in my panic. He instead tightly wrapped his arms around me, small but audible sobs and sniffles bubbling from his chest. No doubt he'd realized what had just taken place. Poor dear, watching his own father, the stoic Halvard Vrana, completely gone and replaced with a possibly malicious and manic madman. I put my own arms around him, securely.

"You will be safe with me tonight, I promise you that," I whispered. I didn't dare let my tears fall into his sight, nor my voice, strangled with emotion, break. "Go pack some things at once, nephew."

⁕

Halvard ran as fast as his aging legs could allow, away from the police, from those accusing him. Another disturbance in his mind took over - a gripping, horrid headache attacked him as he'd attempted to bid his son farewell. He held his pounding head - both sides of his jawline were covered in black. Not a soul trusted him anymore. Had he heard voices from the corridor on the left? No, it was only the abandoned west wing. Perhaps it was the wind whistling through the windows. Cold wind. Snowy air. Perhaps he was going around in circles now. Round and round and round the same hallways. All over the little fortress of a home. Every turn corresponded with another twinge of self-doubt.

"Madness," he thought as he took the right turn. "Insanity," with the left. "Distress," just as he stumbled over something. Halvard stuck out his hands to break his fall. He hit his cheekbone against the corner of a decorative table as he fell, letting out a cry as he landed. Blood oozed from the center of the gash, while a lump began to form. A disgusting, phlegmy cackling filled the empty hallway.

"You!" Halvard fumed as he struggled to get up, eventually getting back on his feet. He blindly let out a bolt of shadow from his hands, then another, and another. The cackling stopped with a cry of shock

"Come, master Halvard, keep your temper," Petimus hissed, clutching his injured arm.

"Not as long as you're here, you vile stain on my home!"

Halvard lunged for the creature, arms outstretched, ready to grab it and pin it down. Petimus dodged with inhuman speed, causing Halvard to fall again.

"Will you not fight me like a man, you revolting creature?!" Halvard yelled into the shadows, watching as the two snake eyes blinked through hiding. "You disgrace, you-you utter, miserable, hellish-"

"Now, Halvard, that's quite enough," Petimus said, swiftly going behind my brother and wrapping his arms around his neck whilst perched on his shoulders. He planted both feet into the man's back to stabilize himself and went into a fit of giggles as Halvard struggled to breathe. "Calm yourself!"

The man fell to the ground again, crying and grunting as he tried to release Petimus' iron grip from his throat. Petimus didn't move, until Halvard began to choke for air, gasping, his face turning a bright red. Now that he was more focused on attempting to breathe, Petimus finally let go and jumped in front of him.

"Shame to see you in such a state," the creature said, watching as Halvard rubbed at his throat, and taking in deep breaths. "You've gotten so angry now. Mad. Poor baby lad, you are."

"I never was," Halvard gasped, "until you...arrived. Now everyone's against me! My family - "

"Oh, and it's such a fun delight to watch unfold!" the thing cackled, "but you've got talent. These powers of yours are impressive. You're becoming more like your mother of the dark."

From the ground, Halvard let out a scream and shot another bolt at the thing, aiming for its neck. He succeeded, then brought the shadows from the ground and wrapped them around the thing's arms, tying them together. The man stormed over to the hissing creature, and picked it up only by its neck.

"You took Nancy, didn't you? And the boys in the city! You took all of them!"

Petimus could only nod through his wet choking and gagging. Black drool oozed from between his sharp teeth. "I'll kill you," Halvard said, "I'll kill you so you won't harm anyone else!"

"Then," Petimus attempted to say. "Nalia...will harm them...herself."

"I'll kill her, too," Halvard hissed, shaking the thing. "Be rid of this plague for good. No one will come near me or my household ever again."

As Halvard spoke, Petimus' hands broke out of the shadow binds. He grabbed Halvard's wrists and dug his claws into them. Halvard dropped the thing with a sharp cry.

"Wretch!" he screamed, pulling the creature by his strings of hair. Petimus yanked itself away, tearing away some of it in the process. He sunk into the ground and arose on a wooden beam on the ceiling.

"You've forced my hand, dear Halvard," he said

from the rafters. "Nalia demands you come to her, and come to her you will."

"I would never!" Halvard shouted into the air.

"Well, then allow me to pay your dear family a visit," Petimus called, the black drool dripping to the floor like rain. "That darling little boy of yours is just the body Nalia needs for her army."

Halvard's heart dropped as he watched Petimus vanish into nothing. And, my friend, you'd best believe he ran as fast as his aging legs could allow.

Chapter 16

"Violet! Violet! Where is my wife?!" Halvard shouted at one of the servant boys. The boy stammered, saying she was in her study. The distraught man ran into the study, where he saw Violet and her ladies-in-waiting packing up her books and dresses to leave. Upon seeing her bleeding, red-faced, panicked shell of a husband, she stood up from her chair. The maids gasped, stunned at the sight. Violet ran straight up to Halvard, ignoring any possible consequences.

"Halvard!" Violet cried, "Halvard, what's happened? Darling, how did you -"

Halvard gripped his wife by the sides of her shoulders. The ladies all let out terrified screams, pleading Halvard to get out and telling Violet to run.

"Where is Sullivan?" the man asked.

"Why - I...I don't know," Violet stuttered as her supposed madman of a husband shouted at her. "The police, dear, you need to go with them!"

Halvard let out a roar and tossed his wife aside. The maids screamed again and immediately rushed to their mistress' aid. Halvard's face went from panicked to outraged.

"I command all of you, find my son at once! Now!"

"Halvard, please, would you compose yourself? I'm begging you!" Violet shouted back.

"Not until everyone in this goddamned house is safe, Violet!" The man crudely wiped the lump on his cheekbone with the back of his hand as he barked orders.

"Why...what happened to you?" the woman sobbed.

"I fell," he said simply. "Hit my head."

"That isn't all!" Violet replied, grabbing hold of his hands.

"Let me go, woman, I'll find my son myself, then!"

"*Halvard!*"

"Get to the coach, darling, do as I say!"

The man was already out the door at the sound of police officers coming from the other side of the hallway.

※

I told Sullivan to pack some of things away at once, so that we could take our leave. The boy, with tears in his eyes, frantically began gathering miscellaneous clothing and books, including, of course, the small Compendium. He shooed Charles out of the room.

"Please assemble the servants and take them to the city," the boy ordered. "Every last one."

"I can't leave you alone, master Sullivan," Charles said, his old voice shaking.

"That's an order, Charles," my nephew demanded through his own tears. "I want everyone...I want them together."

"As you wish."

While the butler left the room and closed the door, Sullivan looked down at his small suitcase crammed with clothing. He felt a heavy weight in his mind, one that sank into his belly. The urgent gripping reality swarmed his head, pushing out all of the fantastical thoughts, the childish awe, the wonder and joy. His father, perhaps the next Ripper? Criminally insane? All under his family's nose, now surfacing at an alarming pace and becoming a danger to everyone! Shattering everyone's image of him! Bringing the whole of his once-peaceful household to tears, panic, confusion! The boy fixed his gaze on the little purple book. In his fit of horrible panic and confusion, he grabbed it and tossed it across the dark room, where it struck something soft.

"SSss!" Sullivan's young heart nearly stopped at the sudden, jarring, snaky sound. "A fine way to introduce yourself, fleshy youth!"

The boy felt a cold and clammy hand clutch at his arm. He pulled it away and shone his candle on the face of the creature on his bed. His breath caught in his throat at the sight of a reptile's eye embedded into a death-ridden human face.

"Oh, hush, no reason to be afraid," said the thing.

Sullivan backed away.

"What - "

"You know what I am," Petimus whispered, holding up the Compendium. "A humble beggar."

My poor nephew put his hand to his mouth, disgusted. Petimus lit the lamps in the room with a snap of his fingers. With the lights coming on, Sullivan could almost fully see the hunchbacked bag of bones. It looked at the boy with his wide, sickening grin. Sullivan turned his head away and gagged at the mere sight.

"Must hurry, there's business to be done, boy. Business with your charming father."

"For ...for what?"

"For the most wonderful woman in the forest, the kindest of hags, the sweetest of shadows. Nalia would love another young man to add to her collection," he added, pinching at Sullivan's healthy and flushed cheek with a not-so-healthy hand.

"I..."

"No need to think about it, boy, you're coming with me whether or not you give it good thought."

The door slammed against the wall as Halvard swung it open.

"Petimus!"

"Ah, speak of the devil himself," Petimus snapped his fingers, allowing a stream of shadow to rush at Halvard. The man fell to the ground with a loud, visceral thud.

"Father!"

The man stretched his arm out.

"Sullivan, move!"

The flickering shadows became one large puddle in the ground. Sullivan stepped away from it as if it were going to swallow him alive. The shadow blob lifted itself off of the ground and covered the creature's eyes with total darkness, like a sudden fog. Halvard grabbed his son's arm and pulled him into the corridor, slamming the door behind him.

"Father, what's happening?" the boy cried. "What was that?"

"Just run!" Halvard shouted, yanking the boy by the arm and giving him a panicked and stern look.

Both the father and the son ran. Their feet slammed against the carpet-covered corridor, heading towards the left turn at the end. Sullivan looked at his sweating father's face, only to notice something dripping down his cheek. The scribbles practically spoke to him - *"I'm bleeding ink!"* As he gazed in terror at his father's extraordinarily rare panicked expression, and as his father took a glance over his shoulder, they both collided with someone. She dropped the garments in her arms and fell back onto her rear. Romilla crawled back, startled.

"Masters, what - "

"Shh, shh!"

Halvard covered Romilla's mouth as an omniscient laugh filled the air. It was a cackling, taunting sound. The master of the house used his arms to push the two youths behind him as he frantically searched for the source of the voice. Petimus rose out of the floor in front of them.

"Courage, courage, courage," he hissed as he rose from the shadows. "How very...noble."

The corpse creature paused before the word "noble" to allow his ever-present smile to finally dissolve into a frown, turning down at the sides of the face. It was hideous. He fixed his disgusting gaze on Romilla.

"You...you aren't dead?"

"Oh, no, please! No!" the girl begged hoarsely, clutching at Halvard's coat. Petimus inched closer to the three, his joints snapping. His voice changed from the sharp hissing sounds to a shrill screech.

"Why aren't you dead?!"

"Petimus, leave her be!" Halvard protested, his arms

covering both his son and his maid. The corpse smiled again, too suddenly.

"Nalia would be most displeased with you, Halvard," he hissed. "Keeping her cold-blooded granddaughter alive."

A wave of shadow charged at the dark man, who shoved the two children further back before being taken down again, hitting the ground hard. Romilla screamed as Petimus came for her, grabbing at her leg, and then at Sullivan's arm.

Black liquid oozed from all over Halvard's face. He could feel it flooding his head, bursting with pulses of pain. Just as he turned around, Romilla took Petimus' vile head in her hand and squeezed it, covering it in a thick coating of ice. Petimus roared in frustration.

"Cold-blooded abomination!" he cursed, slashing blindly at the girl. Sullivan took this chance to pull the girl out of the way and lead her back to his father to help him get back on his feet.

"Look out!" she screeched. This time Petimus brought Sullivan to the ground with shadows, and pinned him there. Sullivan writhed and twisted to break free.

Halvard crawled to his son and pulled him away from the ground. He nearly threw his son back, in order to keep him away from Petimus.

"Bastard!" Halvard blurted. He yanked Petimus off of Romilla and held him by the neck. For a split second, not one of them said a word, and just stared at each other with a raging hatred. With a growl of fury, Petimus bit down on Halvard's arm with his needle-pointed teeth. The man screamed. As he did, Petimus wriggled free and stomped at the ground. He yanked Sullivan's arm and refused to let it go. A black hole opened up underneath the both of them. The creature sank in with his young captive and vanished as quickly as the holes had appeared.

"Pleased to do business with you, master Halvard," Petimus said. "Nalia will be waiting for you."

Halvard watched, his vision becoming red, as Petimus sank into the hole and it closed up.

"Master! Master!" Romilla called, her voice hoarse. He could barely hear her. As blood and black shadow dripped from his face, the man of the house collapsed in trembling defeat.

⚜

Arriving in the city proved to be strange. Violet had promised me that she would arrive with Sullivan shortly after me, but I'd not seen them or their coach yet. I quickly threw money at the nearest inn, ordered my coachman to lead my family into there, and disappeared into the night. Quite a few people stared at me and my coach, whispering amongst themselves. When I entered the pub and called for the bartender, he looked around and slowly approached me.

"Gin and tonic, make it quickly," I ordered, irritated by his sluggishness.

"Beggin' your pardon, sir," the burly man said, sounding nervous. I'd noticed the whole bar grew quiet as I made my order. What a sight it was as I turned around, to see everyone's gaze on me.

"Well, it's about time I'm given some proper respect," I mumbled. No one answered. "At ease," I said again. They turned away and began to lower their voices. I even noticed the occasional finger pointed in my direction.

"Gin an' tonic, sir."

I took the drink and finished it within seconds..

"You must have the most quiet pub in the city," I said to the man. He only grunted in reply.

How surreal it is, to be in a place of merriment, and to see no merriment in the slightest. For god's sake, the little pub seemed as quiet as a graveyard! As soon as it reached my bowel, the drink decided to take it upon myself to create a little noise. To be friendly. To teach these people what a night in the city truly means.

I approached a table of three strapping young women. Two redheads and a blonde. They glanced at each other as I sat down.

"Pardon me for intruding, but I couldn't help but notice how utterly quiet it is in this place," I held up a few coins. "Perhaps with a few drinks we can change this?"

The girls let out some nervous laughter.

"Why, uh - uh, perhaps another time, master Halvard," one said. Insulted, I shook my head.

"You're mistaken, dear."

"Oh."

I suppose, given that we were blood relatives, I could understand the girl's mistake, but that doesn't mean I wasn't the slightest bit irritated. I wanted to hear no mention of that man's name.

"Whatever happened to the girls that disappeared from the Vrana household?" one of the ladies asked.

I scoffed.

"I come to escape those miserable rumors, and this is what I'm greeted with?" I said, my nervous voice rising. "Surely I don't know. They're gone."

"Nancy was a friend of mine," the blonde said. "When your servants asked her mother and father if she was at home, they went on a terrific rampage, asking where their precious daughter was."

I opened my mouth to say something, but struggled. Nancy truly had vanished.

"Well, surely they got the police involved?" I asked.

"The police have been searching, but we haven't heard if they've found her."

"So strange that there's more girls disappearing from that household than anywhere else," one girl said. I could feel more eyes on me. "And you haven't a clue what's happened to them."

I looked around to see a few heads nodding in agreement.

"Why should I?" I shouted, "I'm the only one who

leaves the place. Please, let's change the subjects, darlings. This one is frightfully dull." I put an arm around one of the redheads, who pushed it away.

"Don't you touch them!" an old man in the corner said, standing up. "You'll make them disappear like the others!"

I stared for a moment at the man and then wildly shook my head.

"Wh - see here!"

"Is there trouble here?" the bartender appeared suddenly at my side, grasping my shoulder with a large hand.

"I'm only trying to create friendly conversation!" I stammered. "I've not done a thing!"

"You can't be trusted," the man said. "I'm going to have to ask you to leave here. You're not welcome in this pub."

I'd never been more lost in my life than in this moment. The entire pub stared at me hatefully.

"I won't leave until you explain why!" I shouted. "You can't throw me out for no reason!"

"Then bring back Nancy!" the blonde girl shrieked, tears in her eyes. The rest of the patrons stood up, yelling similar things to me. I shook my head and protested.

"I've done nothing! Nothing, you vile city scum! How dare you treat me this way?!"

"Get out!" they shouted. "Leave our people alone!"

Next thing I knew, I found myself laying in front of the pub, letting the cold snowflakes barrage my face. What in god's name just happened? I stood up, brushed myself off, and sighed. Was the entire city against my family now? Would anyone let me escape the events of my own household, just once?

Someone said my name. I looked up and saw nobody.

"Shandar!"

"Can't you see I'm busy?!" I called back, the sheer misery dripping from my voice. "Do not bother me, or at least get me a second drink!"

I felt a hand on my shoulder.

"Go away, I said!" I waved a hand at the hand.

"Master Shandar, please, this is urgent!"

I turned when I heard the familiar voice. There stood Thomas, the messenger boy that my brother often sent into the city to fetch the doctor. A look of panic overwhelmed his large eyes.

"Thomas?"

"It's Sullivan, sir, 'e's gone. Master Halvard's losing 'is mind."

I could feel a weight dropping in my stomach.

Sullivan was gone.

Chapter 17

"Where is my brother?" I demanded, yanking my coat and hat off when I arrived at home. The maids pointed to the stairs with wide eyes. I could hear shouting coming from upstairs. "Halvard!" I called as I ran up.

Lo and behold, there was my brother, his entire body bent over with the weight of overwhelming grief. He pounded the floor with his bare, bloodied fists. A few servants and the policemen from earlier stood around him, both terrified and in awe.

"Halvard!" I called again. He didn't listen.

"My fault! It's my fault he's gone!" he yelled at the floor beneath him. "I couldn't...I couldn't stop the bastard!"

"Halvard, get a hold of yourself!" I shouted back, approaching him. Violet grabbed my arm as I tried. "What are you -"

"Look," she stammered, pointing at the floor. The shadows flickered around him like fire. I jumped back.

"What in god's name?" I breathed.

"A monster, like me, look!" Halvard shouted. I saw his face for the first time that night, and suddenly felt ill. Black streaks of liquid filled in the creases of his face. The pure rage and grief created such painful wrinkles in his face that made him look twenty years older. All those years of remaining calm in the face of adversity, those years of keeping his thoughts to himself-they surfaced in this time of pure misery, the insanity of losing a child. He let out a few more sobs, then slowly fainted. Violet ran to him.

"What the hell happened?" I asked Violet.

"He...he claims that someone snatched up Sullivan," she stammered, tears streaming down her face. "And he was too late to stop them."

"Have you looked for him? Has anyone found him?"

"We've been looking everywhere, he's nowhere to be found, and now, this. Halvard..."

She attempted to compose herself, but instead broke

down sobbing.

"Do something, you idiots!" I called to the police as my brother's wife sobbed next to me. I felt like the only remotely logical person in the room. The officers clumsily ran off in varying directions. "Please, maybe we can find him! Do something useful!!"

Someone grabbed at my arm. A cold hand, I could feel it even through my clothes. It startled me.

"Master Shandar, I saw -"

I turned to see Romilla's wide, almond shaped eyes. I grabbed her shoulders and disregarded the chill it sent through my body.

"Well, say it, tell me!" I yelled. "Where is my nephew?!"

She backed up, afraid. I did yell rather harshly.

"Romilla, what did you see?" Violet asked, attempting to stifle her sobbing.

"I...the master was right," she said, pointing to him. "Something took him."

"Who? Who was it?"

"A...it was a monster," she stammered. "Like an undead...human," tears formed in her own eyes.

I stared at the girl in disbelief and rage.

"You can't be serious," I said, my voice a low and dangerous hiss. "Answer me with an answer that makes sense, young lady. Who did it?"

"I told you, an undead monster!" she squeaked. "A horrible, vicious monster!" She pointed to the scars on her face. "The one that almost killed me!"

No words. I couldn't fathom what these people were trying to tell me. I sank to the floor and put my head into my hand. The entire world around me was going mad.

"A monster did it," I said. "A monster."

Everyone looked up as Halvard let out a few coughs. We all backed away, in case he threw another fit. He sat up again, letting out a groan from his throat.

"The book, Shandar," he mumbled. "Did Sullivan

have it?"

I went closer to him, my mind in a state of both concern and horrible anger.

"What book?"

"Don't play the fool, Shandar, you know which book!" he shouted, hoisting himself up.

"Not your pretty purple little fairy tale book? You want a bedtime story, you little scab?"

Halvard stumbled back as he stood up. Violet caught him in her arms.

"Search his room, you old bastard!" Halvard ordered. I gritted my teeth and hesitantly went into Sullivan's room, the one we all stood next to. Sure enough, there on the floor was that little purple handbook, opened and face-down. I picked it up and took it out.

"This one?"

"Give it to me."

"Halvard, you idiot, your son is -"

"Give me the damned book, or so help me, you'll be next!"

"Darling, please!" his wife held his arm, horrified.

I handed my brother the book and stepped away. He frantically flipped through the pages, his fingers trembling as he did. He stopped on a page and began mumbling the words.

"Beware the beggar, little one, beware his sharpened gaze. Beware his eyes like a hungry snake, and his touch like torn, rough lace..."

"There's no time for this rubbish," I protested, going to grab the book away from him.

"Shut up and let me read!"

I felt a sharp pain on my forehead as he threw something black towards me. Violet screamed and ran to me, pulling me away. I put a hand to my forehead and felt a slow, warm trickle of blood.

"'Penny for the poor?' he hisses, arm outstretched, 'or a bone for me poor little pup?' Look away, little one,

don't give in to his plea, don't place precious things in his cup."

We looked at Romilla as he continued to read. She stared at the floor, wringing her hands together, in tears.

"...Don't scream as he seizes, he'll do as he pleases, tearing through you with claws made of lies."

"Halvard, this is madness!" I called.

"Beware the beggar, little one, beware all his false claims. Lo, something else lurks, for whom the thing works, the Collector of miserable pain."

"No!" Romilla cried, burying her face in Violet's side.

Someone downstairs let out a hideous screech. Everyone, including Halvard, clambered to the stairway.

"Isabelle, was that you?" Violet called. "What is it?"

Everyone stopped at the bottom of the stairs, where a disgusted Isabelle sat, mouth agape, and something stood in front of the doors. At that moment I realized that "undead" was the absolute best way to describe such a monster.

"Oh-!" Violet gasped, her hand covering her mouth. Halvard pushed past us and grabbed the thing by its arm. As soon as he grabbed it, it tried to sink into the floor through the shadows.

"Romilla, stop him!" Halvard yelled. The girl cried, still clutching Violet's dress. My brother screamed at her again. "Do it!"

Romilla covered her eyes and stomped at the ground. All around the monster's torso, halfway into the ground, turned white-a stark contrast from the black. He stuck to the ground. Everyone witnessing this atrocity recoiled.

"Here is the perpetrator!" Halvard said, in wildly outraged victory. "This disgusting freak of nature, the legendary beggar, the cowardly and hideous minion to the witch in the woods! He's the one that ran off with my dear Sullivan! Where is he, Petimus?!"

The thing smiled. Oh lord, what a repulsive thing that smile was. It nearly split his face in two.

"Safe with Nalia," the thing answered. "For now."

"Bring him back, or I'll tear you apart!"

"Oh, be civil, Halvard, your family is frightened."

"To hell with civility!" Halvard shouted, grabbing the thing by the neck. "Give me my son!"

The maids and servants began to back away, and for good reason. Some were too repulsed to stop looking, including yours truly. Halvard screeching like a wild animal as he interrogated this hellish creature proved too much for us.

"What a lovely family reunion it shall be," the thing drawled. He held out his other hand. "Free me and I'll take you to him."

Violet looked at her husband with terror. He looked back at her, then at Petimus. Oh, the tricks this thing had pulled to draw him to Nalia! He had no choice! The brave man took deep, sharp breaths.

"I'm sorry, Violet," he mumbled, going to her and hugging her. "I'll bring Sullivan back. I promise."

"*What?*"

"I'm afraid no one should be exposed to this dreadful thing in the woods, especially at night," he replied. "Like I was. Romilla, free this creature."

The girl looked down at Petimus, who grinned maliciously at her. She touched the floor next to him and the white went away. Petimus rose from the ground and took Halvard's hand in his own.

"Lovely house, but we must be going," the thing said. Without another word, he and Halvard sunk into the ground.

Violet sobbed for her husband. The rest of the household, admittedly not very many, remained in the spot where he had vanished into the ground. Nervously, I felt that spot on the floor with my hand.

"Solid," I mumbled, still not quite believing what had just happened.

Romilla picked up the little purple book from the corridor upstairs and began to flip through each page.

"Not you too," I growled at her, rubbing my temples with my forefingers.

"That creature was summoned through the book," Charles said. "We should see if there's anything in there that might help us."

"If there's only hideous demons that arise from that little thing, then I want nothing to do with it!" Isabelle shouted. "Right in front of my face! The mere sight alone nearly killed me!"

Romilla looked up at us with a sad, sad expression.

"I can't read well," she mumbled. She held the book up, handing it to me. I pursed my lips and swiped it away.

Violet wiped her face with a lacy hanky. She shook her head as she cried.

"My son...my husband..." she uttered through gasping breaths. "Gone. What if they never come back?"

"We will find them. The police are going into the woods now," Isabelle crooned as she comforted the lady of the house. The sounds of horses leaving our premises came from outside the front entrance.

I sank into a chair in the foyer and began looking through the cursed book myself.

"What do you make of it?" Charles asked, looking over my shoulder.

"What am I supposed to make of it, these child's tales?" I snapped, my eyes glazing over the pictures and the scribblings.

"They aren't children's tales, master Shandar, unless you've not been paying attention to the horrors we all just laid eyes on!"

"Do not raise your voice with me, Charles!" I said, raising my own voice at him though not looking up from the book. "There will be consequences."

"Were these events not consequence enough?! Your brother, your nephew, my masters, the ones I've looked after, vanished into nothing?!"

Shocked, I shut the book and stood up, facing the little man, the one who'd been with our family for decades. His old face turned into one of weariness, of panic.

"You suppose I care naught for my own family?" I shot back.

"You care for nobody except yourself!" The man pointed a wrinkled finger at me. I gritted my teeth in my outrage. I opened my mouth to say something, but he cut off my protests. "Brothels and drinks, night after night, bringing my master Sullivan home ill beyond belief! Forcing him to engage in this behavior only because you wanted to shape him in your own image!"

"Enough!"

Without thinking, I struck the old man with a backhanded slap to the face. Everybody in the room gasped and rushed to him. They all began to shout and protest, but I didn't listen. This is how my family, my brother's household, saw me. I'd rushed home the moment I realized Sullivan vanished, and yet they think I care about nobody except myself. I felt sick. Overwhelmed. Betrayed. And for the first time since I was a boy, I felt burning tears stinging my eyes. I put my hands to my eyes. The protesting continued. Isabelle pushed me aside. Charles shouted his distrust with me. The angry voices of the house consumed my mind, along with the loss of my brother. My nephew...oh, my darling nephew.

Defeated, I hung my head. And I began to cry. I sobbed. I put my head into both hands and let the tears pass through my fingers. Slowly, the maids and servants went quieter and quieter as they watched the tears leak through my hands and drip onto my clothes. Clearly, they were shocked at my expense.

"Master..." Isabelle whispered. "Oh, Master Shandar..."

"Don't say a word," I whispered between sniffles, holding up my hand. "I'm going to find them in those cursed woods. No need for petty squabbles."

"Shandar, we can call for more help," Charles said. "I'm sorry. I'm so sorry."

I'm unsure of what sort of feeling came over me that night. A need to prove myself, perhaps. A desire to show these people that I, indeed, cared for my family.

"Do not bring more police out there," I said. "They won't understand the horrors they're up against." I wiped my eyes with a hanky. "We cannot contribute to the losses that have taken place."

"What if we lose you?"

I looked down. Romilla stared up at me, her eyes full of tears and concern.

"Then I will have died fighting for them," I said. The girl wrung her hands. A wave of cold air blew through the hall as if through an agape window. I looked at her eyes - those almond-shaped, beautiful little brown eyes. They weren't brown, but a pale, icy blue. I pulled away, startled. Romilla touched a nearby wall. A thin layer of frost formed over it. The servants mumbled and took a step away from her and I.

"I can't do much," the girl said, creating circles of frost in the wall, swirling into dazzling shapes. "But I too, would be willing to die for what I love. Like my mother for me."

"And I," Violet said, stepping forward to us. "I shall bring my family back whether it kills me."

We stood there, silent for a moment. I grabbed hold of that little book.

"Isabelle, Charles, and everyone else," I called. "Everyone here is to take shelter at the Morris Inn in the city. Fetch us the warmest possible coats for our journey."

Chapter 18

Halvard shivered as he stepped through the snow. His nose became a rosy red, his eyes were teary, and his hands found their way into his pockets to prevent the freezing cold from breaking them apart. Petimus led in the front, and though it became increasingly dark in the woods, Halvard could still follow the slow sound of the cold joints.

Pop-pop. Snap. Pop-pop. Snap.

"Why not just take me to her with your witchcraft?" Halvard said to Petimus. "I need to find my son. And you wouldn't have to guide me."

"Patience, Halvard. Your son is well. Must weaken you so as to avoid any trouble."

As Petimus explained this, Halvard heard and felt both ears let out a simultaneous pop. The black oozed from his ears, much more rapidly than usual. A storm of a headache approached the back of his mind. He stopped and fell into the snow.

Petimus turned to see the man crumpled and on the ground.

"No use stopping now, little blister, we're nearly there," the thing said, mockingly running his bony hand along Halvard's head. Halvard shoved the thing away and got back on his feet. His knees became wet with the snow that stuck to them.

"Is my son there?"

Petimus growled.

"I've already told you, impatient thing," he pointed to a tree up ahead. "See for yourself."

The man squinted to see in the dark. There, on the tree, crudely tied with what appeared to be an old net, was a blond young man, hanging his head.

"Sullivan!" Halvard ran to his son, trying his hardest to completely disregard the cold, the dry skin, the soaking knees. "Sullivan!" he called again.

The boy lifted his head as he saw his father

approach. He blinked away the tears in his own eyes and sniffled back the drippings from his nose. His lips were blue and quivering.

"Father?"

Halvard rushed to his son and ignored the pain that pounded throughout his head. He clutched at his face, kissed his cheeks and forehead, and wept.

"Oh, Sullivan!" he cried. "My son, my son!"

Petimus, who caught up to the man, snickered.

"So sweet," he said in a voice that was the precise opposite of sweet.

"Release him!" Halvard said through sniffles. "Release him and take him back home!"

"You do not order me around," Petimus said, standing on two legs for the first time since he'd been alive. His spine let out a violent crack. "Not when I'm in my own home."

A terrible voice let out a gleeful giggle. Halvard recognized it and his face went from exhausted relief to horrified panic.

"Take him home," he said to Petimus, his arms around his son's shoulders. "Take my son away from this place, I beg of you!"

"A hearty boy he is," said the wheezing voice. "You and the boy. Father and son. Lovely family."

Halvard tore his gaze from his son to see Nalia - the old hag of the woods. She appeared just as hideous, wrinkled, and cruel as the night he'd first seen her. Halvard released his grip from his son and faced the short, hunched-back old woman. He held his arms behind him in an attempt to protect his son.

"Get him home," he whispered to Nalia. "I'm here now, you do as you will with me."

"Father, wait-" Sullivan protested through blue lips. Halvard shushed him.

"Don't know, would make a lovely one," Nalia drawled, approaching the father and son. "Beautifully young and strong. He'll serve well."

"I won't let that happen, just bring him home!"

"Might spill to others what he's seen," Petimus said, coming towards them from the other side. "Can't bring attention to the woods."

"Correct," Naila affirmed. "May keep him here for now."

"No, please," Halvard begged, "It's me you want! Do you not remember?! Me! I'll do whatever it takes, just take him home! To the city! I beg you!"

Nalia grabbed the hand of Halvard. Black shadows arose from her hands and clasped around Halvard's wrists, ankles, and neck, and covered his mouth. He looked back at his son as Nalia wandered off to her cabin. Petimus let out a horrible laugh.

"Oh, he's said it! Oh he's done it, mistress, he'll do whatever you say! Ahahaha!"

"Stay with the blond boy, Petimus. Halvard is mine. You watch him. Make sure he makes no escape."

Halvard fought back tears. He could hear his son's voice getting distant, calling out to him.

"Father! *Father!*"

I realized the moment I'd asked for my coats just how aimless I was in this heroic endeavor. I could very well be leading my dear sister-in-law and little Romilla into horrible danger. Perhaps it would be best if we brought along others. Not to mention the absurdity of trying to navigate through the forest on our own. It had a thousand horror stories surrounding it for good reason, how were we to make our way through? Were we even certain that the woods is where they went?

Too many thoughts passed through my mind as I dressed for the outside. Everyone chattered and scrambled to get us prepared for the journey. Perhaps there was no time to think or worry - action was needed at that very moment. Who knew what could have been happening to my brother and dear little nephew right then? I shuddered to think of it.

"Master Shandar, what about the police?"

I slipped on my heavy furs and thick boots. Everything my mind spun around like a windmill caught in a storm.

"Tell them to stop their own journey," I mumbled.

"I'm not so sure they'd be of much help."

"They're trained for...for this,," Violet said, though the situation was quite the opposite of what anyone is generally prepared for.

"I'm afraid not even we know what kind of horrible things we're up against," I said to her. "What if we should lose the police in our...erm, struggle?" Violet pursed her lips. "Not to mention Romilla," I said. Romilla looked up at me as Isabelle dressed her in a smaller, heavy coat. The girl's voice trembled, worse than normal, as she spoke.

"It will be an honor, although..."

"Although what, darling?"

"Nalia, the one who wants Master Halvard...she's my...my grandmother."

We all stopped. I lifted my eyebrows.

"What do you mean?" I asked. A rush of frosty air swept the room.

"She...she sent that thing to kill me. She'll be furious if she sees me." The girl began to cry. Dumbfounded, we all exchanged nervous glances.

"Well, surely you've got the power to stop her?" I asked. "Your abilities are...they're extraordinary." How desperate we were to get our family back, putting our faith in this young girl, this poor, terrified young girl.

"She hates me, always told me to stifle my curse," she said through light sniffling. Isabelle offered her a hanky. "It's impossible for me. Happens when I'm frightened. She frightened me so much, I was afraid of myself."

"You can summon ice from nothing," I said. "I saw

it, we all did. With that...that creature. It was incredible."

Romilla shifted her gaze to the front door.

"I...I did," she said.

"Romilla, dear, you are extraordinary," I said. "Dear girl, we need you more now than ever. Please, for me, right at this moment, bring an icicle into your hand."

The girl stared into my eyes. I stared back at hers. I heard the slightest crackling sounds coming from her hands. The Compendium began to grow frosty in one of her hands. In the other, she revealed an icicle nestled in her palm. I smiled and let out a hearty laugh.

"Child, you're incredible! Magnificent! Unlike any I've ever seen!" I shouted. "You need not be afraid of this gift! Embrace it! Cherish it!"

I stopped my celebration when I realized that Romilla's eyes were no longer brown, but a bright, pale blue. And they didn't change. The girl smiled.

"I shall," she said.

"Excellent," I replied.

Chapter 19

Nalia had Halvard's hand in her own. She stroked it and toyed with his fingers as they stepped into her hut.

"Oh, such strong hands," she crooned in an ugly voice, "Powerful. Rich with shadow."

"Against my own will," the man muttered. Nalia tightened the "shackles" on his wrists and slapped his hand. Halvard winced at the sting of old fingers striking his cold and dry hand.

"Truly stubborn," Nalia playfully scolded with a giggle. "Petimus warned me."

Halvard ducked to avoid the glass jars and other trinkets that hung from the ceiling of the low cabin. Nalia led him to a small stool in front of the fireplace.

"Tea?" she asked, forcing him to take a seat. Halvard growled.

"I want no hospitality from you."

Nalia took a ladle full of hot water from over the fireplace and poured it into a handmade wooden cup. She held it out to Halvard.

"Must be cold, dear," she said. "Drink. Regain your strength."

The dark ropes from around the man's wrists dissipated. Halvard only took the cup to warm his hands. He felt his entire body trembling, even from the core of his belly. Not only did being in the presence of the witch terrify him, but her own intense and strong power affected his, like magnets to one another. His entire head swirled with taut pain, as though it were being constricted.

"So strong," Nalia whispered, her hands feeling his face. "Oh, you've grown into such a fine man."

Halvard pulled back, spilling some of the tea.

"Enough of this," he whispered, still trembling. "Please send my son home. Please."

"Perfectly fine," Nalia replied. "That boy will be fine."

"Nalia, I beg you," Halvard hissed. "Do not let him suffer."

"Ha! These woods are perfect!" the woman replied, running her fingers through the man's hair. "No one suffers. Not anymore."

"I suffered, you old hag!"

Nalia's face contorted with black-lined wrinkles. Her face fell as she removed her hands from the man's head. Without warning, she violently knocked into the wooden cup in Halvard's hands and spilled the hot tea all over his lap. Halvard let out a cry of pain.

"Gifted, gifted, you little bastard!!" the woman cried, enraged. "You should thank me! Adore me! Embrace your gift!"

With every exclamation the woman threw something against a wall or into the fire, but never at Halvard. Nonetheless, the man, the tall, dark, stoic, professional man, cowered. For the first time in nearly 30 years, he feared for his life. Nalia, of course, saw this.

"Oh child, you fear me?" she crooned. "You are afraid."

Halvard stood up. He towered over the old hag.

"Just tell me what you want," he stammered. Tears pooled in his eyes. "Kill me if you must."

"Can't kill my vessel," she explained. "Need a man to rule with."

"Rule what?"

"The woods. City. Skadi. The dark midnights of winter. The woods at midnight."

"Is that all?"

"Everyone shall be a shadow," Nalia said, nodding as she stared wistfully out the frosty window. "My shadow. Perfect. The shadows are perfect. We'll rule perfection."

Halvard shook his head. The woman, as he'd determined as a young boy, was completely mad. Mad with her own curse, mad with delusions. Dangerously mad.

"We take them, one by one," Nalia continued,

pointing out the window at a shadow man that lumbered out from behind a tree, a mindless void of a human corpse. "Take the living. Turn them over. Use them to take more of the living. Create a kingdom of perfection. You'll learn to take them. You'll learn."

Halvard recalled this speech from years ago. Boldly, he spoke up.

"The shadows are not perfect," he said. "It's nothing but an affliction. And...and horrible."

"No!" Nalia said, pointing at her vessel, Halvard. "You are perfect! Perfect, do you not understand?!"

"Pain and suffering is not perfection!" the man screamed, losing his own temper. His anger began to completely overtake his fear. Dark droplets trickled down his neck from his ears.

"Then you shall reach perfection!" Nalia screeched. One by one, more shadow people began to appear from the woods outside. They paraded indoors and surrounded Halvard, silently grabbing at him from every angle. While the man desperately tried to fight them away, both with his own curse and with his fists, he couldn't break free. "Take the vessel to the altar," Nalia instructed them. "Bind him to it. He'll see. He'll learn. Ritual is tonight. Tonight!" The woman, as Halvard struggled to break free from the creatures, giggled. "Tonight. Oh, my heart. My dreams. All tonight. *Môj kráľ je doma. Slávny tieňový kráľ.* My love! My dearest!"

Nalia went into her room, her voice soon becoming a fit of hysterical giggling and chuckling and wheezing.

༄

Sullivan shuddered. Violently. He could feel the whole of his face nearly cracking off with the cold, his trapped hands turning red, and the snow soaking into his ankles. His lips quivered, his teeth chattered, his nose dripped...

"Cold, skin-bag?" Petimus taunted as he noticed the boy's horrible shivering. Sullivan could only nod. "I presumed so."

In the near distance, Nalia screamed her displeasure with Halvard, each cry followed by banging and clattering. Sullivan took notice while Petimus cringed at the sound.

"What is she d-doing? To my father?" the boy asked, in broken sentences. Petimus let out a little chuckle.

"She's angry," he stated. "He must not be cooperating." Petimus sat down, cross-legged, on the cold and dead forest floor. A wave of terror and dread filled the boy's mind as he heard a shout, undeniably from his father.

"Why him?" he mustered the strength to ask. "Why my father?"

"He's the vessel," the thing answered as he drew in the light snow with his finger. "Vessel of shadow. Nalia needs him to double the shadows."

"That...that's why he wrote about it. You chased him after... after Nalia cursed him."

Petimus replied with a sharp giggle.

"Hope you said proper goodbyes to him." Petimus continued to draw. His silly lines turned into a head, ears, four legs, and a tail. "Hope you said your goodbyes."

Naturally, Sullivan began to cry with the assistance of the frigid winds and snowflakes.

"Let me," he said. "Let me see him. Please."

Petimus stared up at the boy tied to a tree. He shook his head.

"I'm awaiting orders," the thing said. "Nalia told me to watch you. And here I am." He looked at the spot he'd drawn on. "Dull."

Sullivan, without much else he could do, also stared at the spot. He could make out what appeared to be a child's drawing of a dog. He recalled the poem that had summoned Petimus.

"Your pup?" he asked. "Where is he?"

"Not your concern!" Petimus snapped, brushing

away the drawing in the snow. "Keep your questions to yourself."

Terrified, the boy shut his mouth. Petimus hung his head, then looked up at the boy, then repeated that motion. *Take something he loves*, Nalia had said. *Listen to the begging of the man and son to be reunited. Least they aren't dead. Not yet.*

Petimus watched as tears of mourning and despair flowed down the boy's cheeks. He thought of Verdorben and the last sound he'd made when Nalia sent a javelin through his heart. He shook his head. Of course, it was all for good purpose. He understood now what Nalia meant.

He also understood what Halvard and Sullivan felt.

Little by little, Petimus pulled sticks and fallen branches in front of Sullivan. He then, unfazed by the heat, pulled a flaming branch from Nalia's fire and managed to light a tiny fire for the boy. Sullivan continued crying, as though he'd barely noticed. Petimus sat back down in the cold snow, next to his clumsy creation.

"Keeping us warm," he mumbled as Sullivan cried. "Don't thank me."

Chapter 20

I couldn't even begin to describe my feelings as we journeyed into the woods, the legendary, horrible, frightening Reditum forest. I suppose the first few things I noticed were the cold, the dark, and the miserable sound of our feet crunching through the snow, sticks, and dead leaves.

"You're certain this is the way?" I asked Romilla, who led us through the winding paths of the woods.

"No," she answered. Violet and I stopped in our tracks.

"You mean to tell us we're wandering aimlessly?" Violet asked. Romilla turned around and shook her head. She pointed to her forehead.

"When I feel a terrible pain in my head, we'll know it's closer," she said, then continued to walk, though slower.

"I don't understand," I said. "Is it to do with your... abilities?"

The girl nodded.

"My grandmother, Nalia, has strong powers," she explained. "Whenever she got close, I suffered."

Violet and I looked at each other.

"Romilla, dear, will you be suffering here?" Violet asked with motherly concern. "Had I known, I never would have agreed for you to come along. I shouldn't have in the first place."

"I must," the girl said as she stepped over a fallen log. "If I were to stand aside, I wouldn't be able to protect you."

"You're a brave girl, dear," I said, shaking my head. "All too brave."

Romilla looked at me. Her lips quivered, her eyes watered, her face was red. She sniffled.

"I'm terrified," she whispered.

Violet rushed to her and wrapped her in her arms.

"You poor thing," the woman said, beginning to tear up herself.

I decided not to mention the fact that we had no plan of action for confronting this old hag. Were we to politely ask her if she would release our dear Halvard and Sullivan? Should I attempt to charm her with my looks and charisma? What kind of power does this woman have? Will she attack us on sight? How angry will she be if she were to see us?

"Romilla!"

I looked to see Violet holding the girl, who'd fallen with a light moaning sound. The girl clutched at her head with one hand and cringed.

"Romilla, are you all right?" I asked, rushing to her side. I took the girl from Violet's arms and lifted her from under her shoulders. The girl nodded and gently pushed me aside.

"Getting closer," she mumbled, pointing forward. "And she's performing...something. Must hurry."

We continued into the night as the dread began to truly settle into my stomach.

☙

Sullivan and Petimus still sat in the same spot as the little fire began to diminish quickly with the wind and the snow bombarding it. The boy continued to sob, now hoping that the tears might warm his face despite near-freezing to his cheeks. Petimus paced back and forth on all fours.

"Oh, please, would you kindly stop that pitiful whining?" the thing growled at Sullivan. The boy sniffled. "You're grating on what's left of my hearing."

"I shall do as I please," he replied, absolutely convinced that he was going to die in that spot. "Being so close to freezing to death."

"You know nothing of that, living with your posh furs and large sheltered home," Petimus snapped. "Now if you would shut up."

"Why?"

Petimus stepped through the fire until he stood in

front of Sullivan, and brought himself back up on two legs. What a horrific sight, may I add.

"You'll be in deep trouble otherwise," he hissed, baring his teeth and showing off his claws. "Remember what happened to that disgusting creature, Romilla." Sullivan turned his face away as the hideous claws brushed against his face.

"What did you do to her?" he asked, rather stupidly. Petimus took a moment, let out a snaky hiss from between his mangled teeth, and swiped at Sullivan's face. The boy let out a cry as the claws pierced and tore through his red and chapped skin. Petimus backed away with howling laughter.

"I could do far worse, boy, but I'm waiting for Nalia," he said. "Now don't say another word."

Sullivan didn't. He focused instead on what appeared to be rustling coming from somewhere around them. Petimus noticed as well, looking around for the source.

"Dreadfully hungry," he whispered. "Perhaps a snack. Perhaps my supper." He pushed away dead shrubbery in search of the sound. "Little rabbit, or baby deer, maybe. Must find you, where are you?"

A quiet fizzling suddenly filled the little clearing. Before he could react, Petimus found himself careening towards a thick tree trunk, then frozen to it. Emerging from the darkness was Romilla, Shandar, and Violet.

"Mother!" Sullivan whispered as Petimus cursed and screeched. Romilla waved a hand in front of his mouth to freeze the corpse's lips together. "Uncle!"

"Oh, my son!" Violet whispered in reply, seeing her freezing and bleeding child and rushing to him. "Sullivan, are you all right? Oh, my son!"

I took a burning log from the little campfire in front of us and held it up to the ropes of the net. It began to sizzle and crackle, taking a moment to burn through. I started ripping through the ropes, not caring how hot and blackened my hands got in the process. With the help of the two ladies, we tore through it, and my darling nephew broke free. Violet threw her furs over him.

"We're taking you home," she cried, the tears streaming down her face. "Oh, Sullivan!"

"But father!" he said through shuddering breaths. "What about father?"

"We'll think of something, we have to," Violet replied. "Let me wipe that blood from your face."

A loud crack broke the quiet night. Petimus attempted to break free, without any luck.

"Cold blooded little scab," he muttered through frozen lips. I approached the thing as bravely as I could.

"My brother. Where is my brother?" I demanded quietly. Petimus said nothing in reply and instead stuck out his snaky tongue, caressing my face with it, I pulled away, disgusted.

"He must be in there," I said to my family, pointing to the hut. "We need to infiltrate it somehow."

"Th-the woman is mad," Sullivan stuttered. "She'll kill us." I looked at Romilla, who fell to her knees in the snow, moaning in pain. I went to her and hoisted her up.

"Sullivan, tell me how the legend goes," I said. "The legend of the hag."

"Takes...travelers," he said. "Under the guise of kindness."

"I'm traveling, am I not?" I said. The idea began to form in my head. Of course, I could put my charm and looks to use now. "I can entrance her."

"Oh, Shandar, that's utterly ridiculous," Violet said. "Surely you don't think this...this witch will believe you're just a traveler?"

"And why shouldn't she?" I asked. "Look, I'm going to go in. When I've gone in, I'll see if Halvard is inside. If he's not, search around the place."

"Shandar, please, this is such an awful idea-"

"Violet, my brother's life is at stake," I said, "Please

don't tell me what to do! I'm going to try it. If I fail, Violet, you take Sullivan home, and Romilla, please do what you can to rescue Halvard."

"Shandar!"

I already put on my act, calling into the night for "help". I motioned to the others to step away and hide. Violet began to tear up, as did Sullivan.

Chapter 21

Nalia hummed to herself as she got herself dressed into her best feather cloak and jewels stolen from her victims. Two shadowy figures pulled her hair back and tied it up. The woman cackled.

"Why thank you, darlings," she said, waving a hand to dismiss them. "No more. I look lovely enough."

The shadow people vanished into the floor. Nalia stared into her dirty mirror in admiration. "I'm prepared," she said with an excited giggle. "This will be my finest night."

The woman heard a sound - a melodious and deep voice, desperately calling for help, for shelter, for food. The voice shuddered and broke through the cold. A knock came at her door.

"Of all times," she muttered. "But another shadow. Could always use another." She went into the front and cleared her throat. The woman opened the door to see a tall, thin, handsome, long-haired man in front of her.

"Lost?" she said in her best "innocent" voice. I nodded.

"Pardon me for intruding," I said humbly. "I'm horribly lost. My horse ran off into the night."

"Must be cold," the woman said, feeling my hand. She looked over me up and down. To my relief, her eyes showed the glint - the one I've seen all too many times. The one that interested women often demonstrated. I did my best not to smirk as I ducked into the very small hut. Unfortunately, I did not see my brother anywhere. Maybe she'd hid him in another room. Or worse yet, left him outside like she had with my nephew.

"Please, I'm so terribly lost," I said as the woman in feathers poured me a cup of tea. "And cold, and hungry."

"I'll take care of you," she said. "Must rest and regain strength. Find home tomorrow." She handed me the cup of tea.

"My, you're charming," I said through shivers. "And so kind." The woman let out a raggedy giggle.

"Drink up," she said. "Need warmth and rest."

"What sort of tea is this, if I may ask?" I said, giving it a sniff. Bitter and sweet. Dark maroon stained the light wood.

"Umbraberry, good and strong," the woman replied, sitting next to me in a stool. She invited me to sit in the cot. I raised an eyebrow and remembered my nephew's voice.

Umbraberries are deadly.

"Why, I've never heard of such a berry," I said. "You're an intelligent one."

"Drink up," the witch said. I noted a hint of annoyance in her voice, so I pretended to sip the poisonous tea.

"Oh, lovely," I mumbled. A line of red ran over my top lip. "Pardon me."

Nalia stood up and pulled a little cloth from her table, knocking dust off of it.

"Must forgive me," she said. "It gets awfully dirty."

I wiped my face and toyed with the cloth between my fingers.

"You know, miss, I've never seen someone with eyes such as yours," I said, not lying in the slightest. Thin black lines rushed into the color of her eyes, and then back out. I stared into them, in awe. "Such lovely things, they are."

"Why, young man-"

"How hearty you must be, living here on your own," I said, standing up and towering over her. "And how lonely. Have you no family, no friends?"

"All gone," she replied, now fully focusing attention on me. I smiled my signature smile and leaned down.

"You poor, poor darling," I said, pretending to take another sip of my tea. "I'd be more than delighted to keep you company for the night." I put my hand on her face and ran it to her neck.

Nalia let out another giggle.

"Oh my," she said. I smirked. What a dangerous game this was. But, like any game, it proved to be - somehow - enjoyable. A thrill. Perhaps I'd be dead by the end of it. "Your name, dearie?"

"Shandar," I crooned, running a hand through her hair. "And my, would I love to hear it on your lips."

Perhaps going too far, I sat the old hag down on my lap and began to caress her thigh with my long and pale fingers.

"Naughty boy," Nalia whispered, her old and wrinkled hand finding its way to my own neck. Nervous at her action, I pulled away.

"Make me most comfortable," I whispered, holding her hand and playing with her fingers. I felt a chill come through the slightly open door.

"Oh, I shall," she giggled, standing up and shutting the door. "I certainly shall."

I chuckled, mostly from nerves, but never broke my character or charm.

"Good girl." I truly wondered if this were to be my end. Death by entrancing a dangerous witch.

A loud sound came from outside the door.

"Mistress, mistress, open!"

The woman and I jolted out of our moment, and I from my act entirely. Petimus had broken free.

Nalia opened the door to see her bruised and icy minion jumping and screeching. I prepared to run, though there were not many places to escape.

"With them! With Halvard!" the thing screeched and hissed, pointing at me. "Halvard's brother! He's come to take him away!"

Nalia turned to me, the enchanted glint in her eyes turning to intense fury.

"Is this true?" she asked in a low and dangerous voice. I attempted to swallow my own horrible fear. I shook my head.

"I've no clue what that...that imp is saying," I said,

hardly able to form a sentence. She stared at me as Petimus cursed from the doorway.

"Little bastard!" he screamed. "Nalia, he's come for Halvard!"

"Silence, you horrible blister!!" Nalia shot a long rope of black from her hand, striking Petimus with it. The thing stumbled backwards and fell to the floor. "I shall see for myself."

I put my hands up.

"I've...I've not any idea what that thing meant," I stammered, all confidence gone. "Not the foggiest inkling."

The woman narrowed her already narrowing eyes.

"You certain?" she asked, her voice low and raspy. I felt something constricting my wrists.

"Most certain," I replied. "Absolutely."

Nalia smiled at me, showing her brown and red stained teeth. Without warning, a sharp pain shot through my shirtsleeve and into my arm. I let out a yelp. Nalia held up a bloodied finger as I felt the warmth trickle down to my fingers. The woman then licked her finger clean. My cold breath caught in my throat as her tongue wrapped around her finger and she stuck it into her mouth. She smacked her lips and grimaced.

"Halvard's kin," she whispered. "Thought Petimus had gone mad."

I began to back away, desperately hoping that the others would have reached Halvard by this point. Oh, what a way to die.

"And you thought to fool me?" she hissed, the black in her eyes starting to overtake them. "You dared fool Nalia, boy?"

"I..." There was no talking out of this, so what I did instead was I sprinted for the door. The things on my wrists caught me and I fell to the ground. Nalia stared over me.

"Trapped now, little Shandar," she said, kicking me in the forehead. "You'll die soon enough. Umbraberry tea is poison. Come, Petimus, you hideous thing! And do not say a word!"

Nalia shut me into the hut with a cackle. I couldn't believe she'd not killed me right there. My breathing got faster as I tried to break free from the shadow cuffs that held me back. It felt as though they were chained to the ground.

A chill came through the door again. I looked up, frightened that it was Nalia again. A small hand cautiously opened it.

"Master Shandar?" a small voice whispered.

Romilla stepped into the hut. I couldn't have been happier to see her as she dissolved the strange chains on my wrists with her own power.

"You truly are extraordinary," I whispered to her. "I thought for certain I'd have died."

"I'm here," she said. "We need to find the others, quietly. My grandmother is planning something dreadful, I'm sure."

"And Petimus told of us," I said, standing up straight and rubbing my wrists. The cut on my arm continued to sting. "Come along, quickly."

We rushed out of the hut and carefully followed Nalia's footprints as she and Petimus vanished into the dark ahead of us.

Chapter 22

Halvard could feel his muscles weakening both with the cold and the amount of struggling he did to break free from the horribly strong shadowy bonds. It was to no avail, and thus he gave up entirely.

Being tied to a snow-covered stone altar is quite likely one of the least comfortable things Halvard had ever experienced, besides his first ritual with Nalia. His entire back became soaked with melting snow, and the cold stone certainly helped nothing. He let the snow fall into his eyes, staring straight up into the pitch-black sky through the conifer trees. The man felt an intense headache assault his mind. He looked to see two figures emerging from the dark.

"Father!" one called. Halvard shook his head as best as he could.

"No, no, stay away!" he protested as his wife and child approached the altar. "Run back home, Nalia is coming!"

"We're getting you out, Halvard!" Violet cried as she went up the short staircase.

"I tell you both, leave now or she'll find you and kill you!" Halvard yelled. "Worry about your own safety, not mine, please!"

"Father, please, we must take you home as well!" his son exclaimed. Halvard felt an excruciating pain erupt in both ears. He screamed. Violet nearly stumbled off the staircase. Halvard let out another scream. Sullivan covered his ears, petrified with fear. As he turned from his father and mother, he saw a large group of dark figures emerging from the woods around the clearing. "Mother?"

Violet looked at the woods, where shadow people walked slowly towards the altar. They moaned and mumbled, and the odd one howled like a wolf. Violet pulled Sullivan up closer to her and they stood in front of Halvard, who whimpered as the pain seared through his head.

"Brave little family, eh?!"

Nalia and Petimus came towards the foot of the altar. Petimus laughed.

"Come to watch?" Nalia asked, coming towards Violet and Sullivan.

"Leave them alone, you miserable woman!" Halvard screamed from the altar. "Please, I beg of you!"

"Not possible," Nalia said as she looked up at the Vranas. "No mercy for those that interfere." She shoved Violet out of the way with force that shouldn't have been possible for a woman of her size and age. Petimus jumped onto Sullivan's back and dug his claws into the boy's shoulders. Sullivan let out a cry.

"Don't you touch my family!!" Halvard screamed. Nalia smirked and kicked at the fallen Violet. She kicked harder and harder until Violet rolled off the edge of the short altar. She fell into the snow with a cry.

"Violet!" Halvard shouted.

"Hold her down!" Nalia ordered her shadow people. "Petimus, toss that boy to the shadows."

Petimus did as he was told and yanked Sullivan off to the side, where he hopped off the boy's back and shoved him into the snow on the other side. Both Violet and Sullivan tried to fight off the slow shadow people that grabbed hold of them.

"No mercy for the perpetrators!" Nalia screeched to her people. "No mercy, I said!"

Halvard listened as his son and his wife began screaming aloud in pain. He sobbed. Black oozed from his ears. Sullivan wailed as a creature bruised him with a blow to the head.

No longer was Halvard's curse stemming from fear. The darkness began to sting-to burn-his ears and his chest. Every ounce of his body trembled. The curse arose now from sheer, pure rage. The man gripped at the sides of the stone altar. Shadows branched from his fingers like blood through veins, or a tree's roots through the ground. Halvard's roaring continued as his own shadows ate their way through the bonds. Nalia nodded.

"My king," she said. "My king of the shadow has arisen!"

Halvard broke from his bonds and sat up. He jumped from the altar with newfound strength and fought off the shadow people.

"Demons!!" he screamed in blind fury. He pulled Violet and Sullivan away and tossed them behind him. He kicked, threw blows, screamed, shot bolts of shadow from his hands, and swung his arms. The rage of a thousand storming seas couldn't match the rage of my brother on the night Nalia threatened his family. And yet, not a single shadow man lifted a hand in protest.

The woman and Petimus stood motionless on the altar until Halvard had taken down every shadow man in sight. Triumphant yet exhausted, Halvard collapsed.

"Run," he said hoarsely to his wife and son. "Run away. Now, I said, *now!*"

Violet and Sullivan ran off in the direction of the hut. Nalia chuckled.

"Oh, master Halvard, you've proven your worth to me tonight," she said, standing over him. "Proven so much worth."

A rush of pain flowed into Halvard's mind again. He clutched at it, still breathing heavily from his burst of rage. Nalia put her hands up to his head. Halvard screamed.

"My king," she said, conjuring a black crown and setting it onto his head. "My beloved shadow king. You are mine. Mine!"

The pain - oh the indescribable pain that Halvard felt. It instantly weakened his knees, his arms, his everything. He fell to the ground. Nalia giggled, then laughed, then maniacally cackled. A swirl of black covered the altar as she pierced Halvard's skin with her fingernail. A small storm formed in that black cloud, and tens of thousands shadow people fell from it.

"My people," Nalia said to the crowd of shadow people. "Ravage the region! Bring all the living to their knees in my name!"

Petimus tugged at Nalia's cloak. Nalia looked down at him and sniffed the air.

"You...you smell that?" she asked him. Petimus nodded and backed away. Nalia looked off into the distance. There stood a tall, handsome man, and a small, native girl. "Cold blood," the witch whispered.

༺༻

Never in my life have I seen a woman as furious as Nalia in this moment. Her blazing eyes nearly shot a hole through the skull of her thought-to-be-dead granddaughter. With ungodly speed, she appeared in front of us and grabbed hold of Romilla by the throat. I felt the clammy, cold hands of Petimus grabbing my own and yanking me backward.

"Petimus was supposed to murder you," she hissed into her granddaughter's terrified face. "Maim, murder, mangle, utterly obliterate! You aren't dead! Why aren't you dead, you burnt little scab?!"

Nalia threw her screaming granddaughter to the ground and began to kick at her with all the strength she could muster. I watched helplessly as Romilla attempted to get up and fell back down, while her grandmother screamed obscenities at her. When Romilla remained on the ground, Nalia pointed to Petimus and I.

"You!!" she screamed. "Petimus!"

The creature, unable to disobey, let go of me and walked towards his mistress, staring intently at the ground. Nalia scooped him from the ground and held him up to her face.

"You've failed me for the last time!!" she screamed, throwing him against a thick tree trunk. A horrendous cracking accompanied by a visceral thud filled the air. I quickly helped Romilla up.

"I'll take care of this filthy creature myself!" the woman screamed as the moonlit shadows of the tree began to surround her. She rushed towards Romilla and I with blackened hands and eyes. I shut my eyes and raised my arms in defense.

"No!"

The woman crashed into something and stumbled backwards. Romilla stood with her own arms up, holding a thick sheet of ice. The girl wasted no time. "Get master Halvard to safety!"

Hesitantly, I did just that, running towards my collapsed brother. The shadow people stood up from the altar and stared at me with their dead eyes, then began to lumber towards me. In a panic, I shook Halvard's limp body.

"Hal!" I yelled, ripping that awful black crown from his head. "Halvard, please! Get up!"
The shadow creatures closed in on us. I dug into the ground under my brother's arms and tried my best to lift him up. I felt a creature grab me from behind, and I yelped.

"Crown!" I heard someone yell. Petimus rose from the ground in front of us. "Give him the crown!"

"Get away!" I kicked the thing away. He grabbed at the black crown and held it up to the shadow corpses.

"Your king is here!" Petimus shouted, then affixed the crown to Halvard's head. It attached itself to my brother's head. A shadow man grabbed me from behind, causing me to drop the limp, weak body of my brother.

"No, please!" I begged, my own desperate voice unrecognizable. Halvard began to stand up, in a motion much like the creatures that laid their hands on me. My brother turned around, his eyes pitch-black.

"Let him alone," he ordered. I fell to the ground. Petimus giggled nervously.

"Master Halvard, please -"

"Silence!" Halvard replied, letting a black bolt effortlessly glide from between his fingers and Petimus' face. The beggar didn't give up.

"Kill her," he begged, "kill that witch. She took me pup. Please, my king, please!"

We all looked at Nalia, who had Romilla's neck in her hands again.

"I'll rid myself of you in the most horrible way possible!" she cried out.

"Halvard," I began to say, but he'd already started towards them. The ground there contained a maze of icicles protruding from the ground. Romilla grabbed hold of her grandmother's wrist and let it freeze under her fingertips. Nalia shouted and dropped the girl.

Halvard swept a weak hand at the icicles in his way, breaking them to clear himself a path.

"Romilla!" he shouted. "Get away from here!"

"She's mine, you traitor!" Nalia screeched. "Mine, I tell you, mine!"

"You've given me this crown, witch, and this power, I will do as I please!"

Halvard took both Romilla and Nalia by their wrists and dragged them through the icicle-covered ground. He tossed Nalia down and held Romilla close behind him.

"You've betrayed me!" the woman cried, black tears forming in her eyes. "My king betrayed his queen!"

"People of the shadow," Halvard called into the night, "Your queen has committed crimes beyond measure to the family of the king!"

The lumbering shadows tilted their heads. Petimus let out a fit of disgustingly gleeful laughter.

"Traitors! All of you!"

"Master, wait!" Romilla pleaded. "Please!"

"The damage has been done, Romilla," Halvard said in a softer voice. Nalia wailed aloud, her tears creating black marks in the dirty snow. The zombies of the shadow surrounded the woman.

"Don't kill her, please!" the girl shouted. Halvard let go of the girl's wrist and faced her.

"Why shouldn't I?" he hissed. "After all she's done to me, my family, my household, your mother, you! She deserves nothing but pain!"

Disregarding my brother, the girl threw herself in front of her grandmother. Halvard stared at the girl. For a moment, all seemed far too still, besides the sobbing witch. The man looked at Romilla, who, in his mind, appeared as Jura. Halvard removed his crown as Romilla froze her grandmother to the ground. He looked at it for a moment before throwing it into the snow.

He did not wish to be associated with such horrific black magic any longer.

A primal screech came from behind us all - one that shook me to my core, as though hell had opened up and let the sinners crawl out. Before I had a chance to see what had happened, Petimus assaulted Nalia with all the force he had in his body.

"Death to the queen!" he screamed, donning the crown on his own head. I grabbed Romilla and pulled her away from the onslaught of blows and claw swipes. Nalia let out a series of ugly, choking shrieks. The shadow people, mindlessly following the black crown, began mimicking Petimus with their arm movements, attacking the witch. Black blood spilled from beneath their feet, and Nalia writhed and wriggled until, at last, all of her cries and movements came to a complete halt. As it all happened, the shadows began to fall with loud thuds. One by one, they all littered the ground. Petimus stood atop the body, panting, with bloodied fingers. He looked at us.

"Let this beggar beg no more," he whispered in a crackling, hoarse voice. "I've no one to serve now." The creature plucked a large icicle from the ground, then drove it directly into his own chest with a wail. Romilla buried her face in my side and covered her ears. Halvard and I simply stared in awe. The battlefield was covered with nothing but remnants of a now-extinct cult of shadow.

But most of all, Nalia was dead. And - in an utterly

morbid and twisted way, my friend - I, along with my brother and Romilla, felt utterly relieved.

Chapter 23

We finally heard back from Sullivan after he'd been overseas for months. I loved reading his letters, as did his mother and father. Halvard came into my room that morning with the anticipated document.

"Sullivan's written back," Halvard said, a smile on his face.

"Good news, I hope?" I said, putting out the cigarette I held. Halvard handed me the paper.

"Oh, it's wonderful news just hearing from him," my brother said. "But yes. He's done so much for his company."

I started to read aloud to annoy my brother.

"Dearest Mother, Father, and Uncle, I hope you'll be excited to know that the company will be reaching out to the eastern region of Kvetina. I've been sent on my next assignment there, and will write when I've arrived safely. We'll be merging with their own business to extend sales. As much as I miss the snow and the cold, I've heard many a story about the lush green jungles and hillsides of Kvetina. I do hope that I'll be able to see the fabled landscapes and flower farms. Apologies for the brief message, but I've written this in a bit of a hurry. You will receive another when I arrive. Please do tell everyone that I hope they are well, including Romilla, of course. I sincerely hope the adoption process has finished by now, and that she's officially become a member of the Vrana family.

Best regards and wishes, Sullivan Vrana."

I couldn't help but beam with joy with every single word I read, and from the looks of it, neither could my brother.

"He's come so far," the proud father uttered.

"Indeed," I replied. "About that last bit, though, how is the adoption process going?"

"Taking far longer than we'd imagined it would, the courts find it difficult due to Romilla's native background."

"I would have thought," I said. "When's the next appointment with them?"

"Today, actually," Halvard said, tucking the letter into the inside pocket of his greatcoat. "Would explain the formalwear, would it not?"

"Every day warrants formal wear when you're a Vrana," I chuckled. "Am I invited to this meeting to charm the judges?"

"You can certainly come, but charming the judges will prove to be difficult, I'm afraid."

"Send for Charles, then," I replied. "I'll match your dress today, and we can truly seem like brothers, although you may not want such a thing. I'm surprised you'd like to be seen with me in Asterbury."

My brother let out a strong, hearty laugh.

"I could use the company of a charming man, I've nothing to offer in that regard."

My cheek pulled my lips into my signature smirk.

"Excellent."

༺༻

We'd been blessed with a day filled with sunshine, which of course made the city glow as the snow glistened and every building looked much more vibrant. The court meeting took far too long, and of course, I couldn't win the judges over. Mainly they couldn't find the humor in...well, anything. I could even hear my brother stifle a snort of laughter at one point. I won't bore you with the details of the meeting, however, besides one:

Romilla's hug when she'd been declared a Vrana was one of the most genuine I'd ever had the pleasure of returning.

"I feel a celebration is in order," Halvard said as

we'd walked down the steps of the courthouse. Romilla let out a giggle.

"Agatha and I could make us all cakes!"

"Don't forget the wine," I chimed in.

"Indeed, indeed," my brother said. "I'll tell Violet the wonderful news right away, and then we shall begin planning at once."

As I let my brother and my new niece into the coach, I heard a scuttling sound behind me. I turned to see a woman on her hands and knees in the snow, scrambling to pick up the neat little packages she'd just bought, presumably.

"Let me help you with those," I said. "Charles, I'll be there in a moment!"

"What a gentleman you are," the woman stammered. "I'm so sorry if I've interrupted your departure."

"Not at all," I said as I plucked the fruits and boxes of bread from the ground. "Shame about your groceries, I'll be happy to buy you more."

I stopped. This mysterious young lady tucked a curly lock of deep brown hair under her bonnet. Her eyes were young and jubilant, her clothing humble and cozy, her face round and reddened by the cold.

"That won't be necessary, but thank you anyway, sir," she said. "Sir?"

"Ah, yes, of course," I said, breaking out of my daze. "But, uh..." I turned to see my brother peering at me from the coach. He smirked and nodded. I could hear him tell Charles to bring him to a nearby flower shop. I waved at them slowly.

"You'd best be off, your coach is leaving," the woman said. I smiled as I heard the horses trotting off.

"Don't mind them," I said. "I can walk you home if you'd like. I'd like to know your name."

The woman smiled once again, and looked at the ground.

"I...my name is Clara," she said. What a sweet name, for a sweet girl. The sweetest I've ever seen. An angel among the most beautiful women.

"And mine is Shandar Vrana. May I?" I said, taking a gentle hold of her basket. "Tell me about yourself, my dear."

Clara told me about her life as an aspiring poet, living with her mother, sister, and father. Romilla looked at me from the carriage and nodded with a smile on her face. Halvard turned her around and made a playful "shush" motion.

As for me, I listened. I listened to Clara's gentle voice laugh with my silly quips. I listened to her telling me stories of her family, of her childhood, of her life in a humble little house in the city. I watched her button nose crinkle, her thin lips reveal her pearly whites underneath them.
The coach began to drive away, but I paid no mind to it.

Romilla spoke up to her new father after peering out at me.

"You don't suppose Master Shandar's gone soft?" she giggled.

"Uncle Shandar to you, now," the man replied, taking one last glance at me and the most beautiful woman in the world. "He's always been soft, dear. Soft as a feather pillow."

"I like it," she replied. "He went soft like you!"

Halvard looked at the wide, almond eyes. The eyes that contained a horrible past, the soul that shared so much with him, so much hurt, and so much misery. And yet, my friends, he grinned as he saw them. He grinned, as tears brimmed in his eyes.

"I like it too," he said, pulling Romilla into a fatherly embrace. "Oh, Romilla May Vrana, my dear..."

The girl shut her eyes, which also filled with tears. They rode further into Asterbury, as a young child noticed the coach's wheels leaving behind not only tracks, but beautiful crystals of frost as well.

" "Family need not be defined merely as those with whom we share blood, but as those for whom we would give our blood." " -Charles Dickens